Nicky Fifth
Fit

by Lisa Funari-Willever

Franklin Mason Press
Columbus, New Jersey

For my children, Jessica, Patrick, & Timmy
Special thanks to Dawn Hiltner & Iris Hutchinson
Special thanks to Dr. Lisa Seed

Many thanks to The Horizon Foundation for New Jersey for your support of this title and the well-being of New Jersey's most precious resource, our children. Your tireless work to bring quality health and wellness programs across the state will make this the strongest, most well-informed generation yet.

Franklin Mason Press ISBN: 978-0-9857218-5-5
Library of Congress Control Number: 2016912126
8 7 6 5 4 3

Editorial Staff: Amanda Barnett, Iris Hutchinson, Stephanie Eppolito, Jessica Willever, Patrick Willever, Tim Willever, Jen Wahner, Marcia Jacobs, Dr. Lisa Seed, and Ashling Wahner.

www.franklinmasonpress.com
www.nickyfifth.com

Table of Contents

NICKY FIFTH'S
PASSPORT

N**P**F

Visit nickyfifth.com.

Download and print your free Nicky Fifth Passport. Use it when you visit the real NJ locations that the Nicky Fifth characters visit.

The Nicky Fifth Series

Chapter One

Not the Beaties

The moment I walked into my house, I just knew something was wrong. My parents were sitting on the couch and they had a very familiar look on their faces. I remembered that look from when they announced we were moving from Philly to New Jersey. It was definitely not a look I enjoyed.

"Oh no," I said as I stopped moving forward. "What's wrong? We're not moving again, are we?"

"No," my mom shook her head. "We're not moving. Why would you ask if we're moving?"

"Because it looks like something is wrong and you both have that *something-is-wrong-look* on."

"Well, sport," my dad began, looking serious and distracted at the same time. "Why don't you just get your brother and sisters for us?"

"Oh, no!" I gasped. "Did someone die? Is it Pop?"

"No, no, no," my mom said with a small smile. "No one has died. Just go get your brother and sisters."

I was confused and nervous. I couldn't find anyone. I checked my sisters' room, I checked my brother's room, and I checked my parents' room. Just as I was about to give up, I found all three of them – on my bed. I was so worried about my parents' announcement that I forgot to holler at them for being in my room. As quickly as I could manage, I dragged every sibling I had to the family room.

"Are we voting on something?" asked my brother, Timmy.

"I vote for chocolate," said my sister, Maggie.

"No, not chocolate," protested my youngest sister, Emma. "I want *spawberry,* I want *spawberry*."

"If you can't say strawberry, then you can't vote for it," Maggie insisted. "So I win. I pick chocolate."

As my sisters debated the merits of chocolate and spawberry, my dad took a long, breath so deep.

"Kids, your mom and I have something to tell you," he said.

"Hey guys, are we having a family meeting?" said T-Bone as he waltzed right through the front door. "Good thing I ran or I might have missed it."

I saw my mom squeeze my dad's hand. I knew this must be serious. He wasn't yelling at us to cut it out and he didn't even have a snappy comeback for T-Bone. This couldn't be good.

"So, I just wanted to tell you guys, together, that I went to the doctor and she thinks I have diabetes."

"Oh no," Maggie wailed. "You're dying from the *beaties*? That's terrible. Not beaties! Get a new doctor. Tell her she's fired and tell the new doctor to take it off of your report card."

"I have beaties, too," Emma yelled, as she rubbed her head and foot. "Daddy, you gave me beaties."

"Are the beaties contagious?" Timmy asked, now rubbing his foot and wondering if he had caught some deadly infection.

"Now, everybody, calm down," exclaimed T-Bone. "Don't be silly. Of course beaties are contagious. Mrs. A, where do you keep your disinfectant? I'll start wiping the door knobs, light switches, and remote controls. You wipe down the appliances and bathrooms. And don't forget the faucets. You know, people always forget to wipe the faucets."

While T-Bone ran toward the kitchen and before my dad could start yelling, my mom raised her two fingers in the air. This was the same signal she used to quiet her class when she used to teach Kindergarten. Despite the sudden, wild chaos, it worked. Maggie, Emma, and Timmy also raised two fingers in the air and shushed the rest of us.

"Kids," she said, "Daddy isn't dying from beaties."

"Yay! Daddy's gonna live!" interrupted Maggie. "Daddy's gonna live! Let's get him some chocolate."

"Mr. A., you're gonna live!" T-Bone exclaimed as he hugged my dad. "It's a miracle!"

"No," said my mom in her sing-songy kindergarten voice, "I want you all to sit back down, be very quiet, and let us explain."

"Thanks," my dad said as he shook his head. "Kids,

my doctor thinks I have diabetes. It is a disease, but it's not contagious. In fact, many, many people have diabetes."

"Ohhhh," T-Bone interrupted. "I think a lot of actors get that because I see so many commercials for it. I think you'll need a needle every day. Or you won't. You're not afraid of needles, are you?"

"Tommy," my mom tried subtly hinting to T-Bone, "are you sure you're not too uncomfortable, you know, with this being a serious family discussion? If you want to come back later, we would completely understand."

"No way, Mrs. A., in times of trouble, family sticks together," he responded. "I'm not going anywhere."

"Of course you're not," my mom nodded.

"So anyway," said my dad, "there are two different types of diabetes. Type 1 is often diagnosed during childhood and Type 2 is diagnosed more often in adults. My doctor thinks I have Type 2."

Suddenly, just like we were sitting in a classroom, several hands went up. They were all sitting so quietly, except for T-Bone. He was waving his arm back and forth and making noises. Just when it looked like my dad would call on T-Bone first, he turned to my brother, Timmy, and pointed at him.

"Dad, is Type 2 twice as bad as Type 1?" he asked.

"No," he said, smiling. "It doesn't work that way. Type 2 is somewhat different and treatment often starts with diet, exercise, and sometimes medicine."

My dad scanned the room. Maggie and Emma were still sitting quietly with their hands raised. T-Bone continued to wildly wave his arm in the air.

"Okay, Maggie, what's your question?"

"Can you still run around and play with us?" she said in a very quiet, somewhat nervous tone.

"Sure," he said, with a little chuckle. "I can still do all the things I always do with you guys."

"Can you still pick me up?" asked a sad Emma.

"I'll always be able to pick up my little peanut," my dad said with a wink. "Although, you are getting very tall, so *always* may not be very accurate."

As the hands in the air dwindled, my dad looked directly at T-Bone and pointed to Emma again.

"Daddy, I have a very big question," she began. "Can I get a new doll, a coloring book, and a pony?"

My dad took a deep breath, looked at my mom, smiled at Emma and said, "No."

"Guys, your father and I are still learning about diabetes and we haven't gotten the final word from the doctor, yet," said my mom. "So, let's wait until we have more information and then we'll talk to you about this some more."

"Ah-em," T-Bone fake coughed, his arm growing weaker, yet still waving in the air.

"Oh yeah, Tommy," my dad nodded, "did you have a question?"

"How can you have any kinda diabetes?" he asked. "You're the produce manager of a grocery store. Isn't diabetes about food? Your whole life is about healthy foods, with all of the fruits and all of the vegetables. Shouldn't you be immune to diabetes?"

"I do love fruits and vegetables," my dad began, "but I'll tell you a little secret. I've always had a little bit of a sweet tooth."

"*A little bit of a sweet tooth?*" my mom laughed.

"I want sweet teeth, too," Maggie said as she jumped up and down. "I want sweet teeth and some rainbow hair."

"Me, too," Emma joined in. "Sweet teeth, a new doll, a coloring book, and a pony with sweet teeth."

Before my parents totally lost control of the room, I raised my hand. There was only one question I wanted answered. "Will you be okay, Dad?"

"Absolutely," he said. "As soon as the doctor tells me what I need to do, I'll do it."

"And we'll all do it with you," my mom said as she patted his back. "Who knows, maybe we'll all end up much healthier than we would have ever been."

"I guess," I said, not convinced. "If you're done, we're gonna go outside and plan our next day trip."

"Sounds good, sweetie," she said. "I'll let you know when it's time for dinner."

As we sat on the front steps, T-Bone wondered why I didn't bring a notebook.

"I don't want to plan a trip right now," I said. "I just wanted to get outside."

"Why?" he asked. "What's wrong?"

"What do you mean, what's wrong?" I snapped at him. "You were inside with us. My dad might have diabetes. Didn't you hear what they said?"

"First of all," he began, "I heard everything they said. Your dad may or may not have diabetes and if he does, it's Level 2, and they can treat it."

"Okay, it's not Level 2. This isn't a video game," I corrected him. "It's Type 2. And we don't even know what the treatment is or what this means."

"Then why are you so worried?" he continued. "Shouldn't you wait until you know something for sure before you worry?"

"Do you even understand the concept of worrying?" I asked, growing more annoyed. "People worry about things before they might happen. That's why they call it worrying."

"Not me," he said. "My dad always says 90% of what we worry about never happens, so why worry until you know for sure?"

"So, if you were waiting for medical test results, you wouldn't worry until they came in?" I asked.

"Nope," he said with a nod. "Wouldn't even give it a second thought."

"And before taking a major test, you don't even worry a little?" I continued.

"Nope," he repeated. "Not even a little."

"You just found out a major storm is heading our way," I persisted, "you're not a little worried?"

"That depends. Is there thunder with this storm?" he asked. "I'm not a fan of thunder. Except for the Trenton Thunder baseball team. Then I'm a huge fan of thunder. But not the weather kind."

"Okay, so for a minute, think about it this way," I began. "Waiting to find out about my dad is the same feeling you would have if you thought a thunderstorm was heading our way."

"Oh, no," he said. "You must be a nervous wreck. There's only one thing to do."

"What?" I asked. "Hide under my bed?"

"No, I've tried that before, but you can still hear the thunder," he smiled. "I meant we should do what we always do when we don't know about something - *call Wanda and start Googling.*"

He had a good point. Any time we needed to learn about something, we talked to Wanda and headed to the computer. However, before I could even turn on the computer, Wanda was at my front door.

"Hey, Nick," she said as she came in and plopped her bag on the floor. "T-Bone said we needed to do some research. I was going through some of the suggestions we received from other kids in New Jersey and they have some really great ideas."

"Actually," I said, "this isn't about another Garden State Adventure. It's way more serious."

Sensing the mood in the room, she stopped, sat down, and said, "What's wrong?"

"Mr. A. might have diabetes," T-Bone announced. "And even though most of the stuff people worry about never happens, Nicky is determined to worry about it before the results come in."

Wanda just stared at T-Bone.

"What?" he said.

"T-Bone, that's very normal," she tried to explain,

turning her attention toward me. "Nicky, what exactly did the doctor say?"

"If he has it," T-Bone interrupted, "it's Level 2."

"T-Bone, they don't have levels in diabetes, they have Types," she corrected. "There's Type 1 and Type 2. Depending upon the type, treatment could be medicine and lifestyle changes, like diet and exercise, or it could be just diet and exercise. There's no reason to panic."

"How do you know so much about diabetes?" I asked. "Before today, the only thing I knew about it came from commercials."

"My third grade teacher and one of my classmates had diabetes," Wanda explained. "And our teacher, Mrs. Bretz, was awesome. She explained things so we could really understand it. She literally drew us pictures on the whiteboard, and even read us some books about it. She said there is nothing scarier than fear of the unknown, *even diabetes.*"

Wanda was right. I was worried about a disease my dad may or may not have and, even if he had it, I knew nothing about it. Luckily, my friends were there to help me out. No one could research like Wanda or distract like T-Bone. *No one.*

The rest of that day was kind of a blur. The news didn't seem to affect my dad too much, except that instead of a giant bowl of ice cream after dinner, he ate a medium bowl of grapes. While I tried to take T-Bone's advice and not worry until there was a reason to worry, I was definitely worried. I did, however, know T-Bone was right about one thing: information was the best way to fight fear. Luckily, we were all handy with research.

The next day I was filled with thoughts of diabetes. During my first three classes, I desperately tried to concentrate. Unfortunately, all I could think about was getting home and reading everything I could about it. By fourth period, I decided to visit the nurse. I arrived complaining of a headache, but I had an ulterior motive.

"So what brings you here?" asked Mrs. Leary.

"I think I have a headache," I said, nervous she would know that I was lying.

"Uh-huh," she nodded as she pulled my file. "When did it start?"

"Oh, um, I think it was, um, like some time this morning," I mumbled, definitely aware that lying wasn't my strong suit. Keep it vague, I told myself.

"You eat this morning?" she asked, taking notes and avoiding eye contact. I decided as long as she didn't look directly in my eyes, I would be fine.

"Um, do you, mean, um, breakfast?" I stammered.

Suddenly, she turned her head in my direction and looked over her reading glasses. The moment I had dreaded had now arrived: eye contact.

"Nicholas," she said without blinking, "is something else wrong? You seem a bit nervous."

"Who? Me? Nervous? No, not at all, I just have a stomach ache," I tried to expertly cover my tracks.

"So your headache suddenly dropped down to your stomach?" she quizzed, now squinting at me.

"I meant to, um, say that I, um, have a headache," I whispered, positive that she knew I didn't have a headache. Ironically, my stomach was actually starting to hurt from all of this stress.

"Okay," she said as she placed her file and pen on the desk. "What's up?"

It was too late. I had two choices: run out of her office as fast as I could or tell her the truth. I was too queasy to run so I opted for the truth.

"I don't have a headache," I confessed. "I just wanted to ask you about diabetes."

"Hmmm, diabetes," she nodded with a smile. "Wanna tell me more?"

"It's not me," I began. "But my dad's doctor thinks he may have diabetes. Level 2, I mean Type 2."

"Okay," she smiled. "The first thing you need to know is that diabetes is manageable. If your dad does, indeed, have diabetes, his doctor will then determine, based upon the numbers on his tests, if he needs to change his diet only or change his diet and take medication."

"I figured that," I said. "I see all of the commercials for the needles."

"Actually, you're getting a little ahead of yourself," she continued. "Not everyone uses needles every day. Some people, depending upon their numbers, can take pills."

"Really?" I asked. "I didn't know that."

"There's so much you don't know at this stage," she

said. "Knowing that your dad can manage it, I would wait until he sees his doctor, gets all of the information, and then he can explain it."

"So you think he'll be okay?" I asked.

"Not only that," she smiled. "But, in my experience, when one family member gets diabetes, it brings the whole family closer, and that often makes the whole family healthier."

"My mom said that, too. But, how can my father being sick make us healthier?" I wondered.

"Well, once the whole family starts to pay attention to nutrition, they make healthier choices," she said. "And, often, people may not realize they're making poor choices."

"So, if I learn as much as I can about nutrition, I can help all of us? Including my dad?" I asked.

"Absolutely," she nodded. "But a bit of free advice: don't focus on what you can't have. Instead, focus on what you can have."

"Hmmm," I thought about it. "That makes sense."

"I find that people are more successful when they

aren't fighting against diabetes, but living to be healthy," she added. "Now, here's a pass to return to class. Stop by any time you have questions."

As I turned to leave, I saw T-Bone shuffling down the hallway, holding his side and covering his ear. As he passed me, he winked and whispered, "Don't worry I've got this. I'm not sick or hurt. I'm gonna get some diabetes information from Mrs. Leary."

"Too late," I laughed. "I already did the same thing. Except I used a headache."

"Did it work?" he asked.

"Well, she realized I didn't have a headache, but she gave me a lot of good information."

"Great," he said, standing straight. "Wanda and I are coming over after school to plan our next trip."

"Okay," I nodded. "Where are we going?"

"Healthytown!" he exclaimed.

I looked confused. "Did you just say Healthytown?"

"Yup," he said. "First stop, the road to wellness."

And with that, T-Bone returned to his class. I wasn't sure if he had finally lost his mind or if he really was the best friend a guy could have. I figured it was probably a little of both. Thanks to Mrs. Leary, I was a little less preoccupied with my dad's condition and able to get some of my work done. Ten minutes after I walked into my house, T-Bone and Wanda arrived.

"Nicky, I have so much information," said an out-of-breath Wanda.

"Why are you breathing so heavy?" I asked.

"Well," she began, blowing the hair out of her eyes, "T-Bone insists that we can't just stroll down the road to wellness. According to him, walking is missing an opportunity to be more active."

"Why are you jogging in place?" I asked an arm-raising, knee-pumping T-Bone.

"That's simple," he said. "We should really use every opportunity to be more active."

"And you're going to jog in place the whole time you're here?" I wondered.

"No," he said, as he launched into jumping jacks.

"So, anyway," she continued, "I compiled a variety of information and separated it into the following categories: nutrition, activity, stress management, rest, and good and bad choices."

"You did all that since yesterday?" I asked.

"It didn't take long," she replied and pulled out color-coded folders. "I did it in between studying for two tests and writing a report. No big deal."

"I hate to bring this up, especially after you did so much work," I began, "but diabetes is mostly about nutrition. I think you might have done way more research than you needed to."

"Correction," T-Bone said in between sit-ups. "The road to health is more than nutrition. Everything she said is important. I was thinking about it, Nick. When you first moved in, we used to always play ball with all of the other guys in the neighborhood. Then we became *New Jersey's Unofficial Junior Ambassadors* and we became less active."

"I guess that's true," I agreed. "In Philly, I played baseball every day. My friends and I never sat still, we were always running around. Now we're on the computer or in the car a lot."

"Exactly," said T-Bone right in the middle of what appeared to be a strange yoga pose. "We need to find a way to fit in more activity every day."

"That's a good point, but let's start with nutrition first," said Wanda. "All day long we're faced with choices about what we eat and drink. My mom always says it's easier to make those healthy choices in the afternoon if you've start by making healthy choices first thing in the morning."

"I agree," said T-Bone, now standing on his head. "For wellness, nutrition is definitely a biggie."

"Well, the only problem is," I countered, "we're hardly experts on nutrition. We're not doctors. My mom is always talking about how we're bombarded with commercials for unhealthy foods that make us think the foods are healthy. It seems so sneaky and dishonest. How will we know?"

"True," said T-Bone. "That's why we shouldn't just try to figure out how to keep *us* healthy."

"You're not suggesting..." I began as T-Bone smiled and nodded his head.

"That's exactly what I'm saying," he continued. "We can be *Unofficial Ambassadors of Wellness*."

"Now, I think you've really lost your mind," I sighed. "If we can't figure out what's healthy, how are we supposed to tell other kids?"

"Hold on," Wanda said as she looked up. "I think T-Bone is actually making sense."

"See," he said, "Wanda thinks I'm making sense."

"Well, we have something that people didn't have before," she replied.

"Smart TV's?" asked T-Bone.

"No, T-Bone, not smart TV's," she said with a sigh. "In the past, people didn't have the internet."

"But everything on the internet isn't true," I said.

"Of course it isn't," Wanda laughed. "That's the biggest myth of the internet. But there are good, solid websites that do provide great information."

I looked at my friends. Wanda was paging through her papers and T-Bone was touching his toes. I suddenly realized that no matter what the doctor said, my dad was in good hands...*even if it was our hands*.

Chapter Two

Healthy Foods, Please Step Forward

It didn't take long for us to start uncovering the kind of information we needed. While there were many inaccurate websites, Wanda was right. If you knew where to look, the internet was an amazing tool. I wondered why more kids weren't using it to learn about really being healthy. But, then I remembered that, until my dad spoke to us, I wasn't exactly taking advantage of it either.

The next day, Wanda and T-Bone came over and, instead of researching great New Jersey places to visit, we planned to research wellness. While Wanda always carried a tote bag, the tote bag she carried today was huge.

"Nicky, can we work in your kitchen?" she asked.

"Sure," I shrugged as I led the way.

She set her bag on the table and started unloading its contents. There were bottles of fruit punch, lemonade, and soda, along with fruit cookies, sugar cookies, chips, fruit snacks and granola bars.

"Wanda, I'm no expert," said T-Bone, "but I don't think all of those things are actually healthy."

"We'll see," she said as she arranged the items in a neat row. "T-Bone, pull the items you think are healthy forward."

"Oh, this is fun," he said, staring carefully at each item. "You should have made this a little harder."

"Take your time," she said as she confidently sat down and made herself comfortable.

"Hmmm," he mumbled. "If I know you, one of these items is probably a trick; like an item I think is healthy that really isn't or an item that I think is unhealthy, but is really good for you."

"Pick something already," I said, growing more impatient by the second. "It's not that hard."

"Or is it?" he asked, totally overthinking it.

After five minutes of intense staring, T-Bone started shuffling the items around the table. He moved some items back and forth six times. In the middle of it, he started bending down and doing squats. Finally, he seemed pretty happy with his decisions and, in the mean time, he'd also warmed up enough to run cross country.

"Are you sure?" Wanda sighed.

"Yup," he nodded. "Hate to brag, but I nailed it."

"Perfect," she said as she handed me a notebook. "Now, Nicky, take this notebook and write down any items you disagree with."

I studied the items and suddenly realized why it took T-Bone so long. This wasn't as easy as I thought it would be. There were some items I just wasn't sure about. I decided to follow my gut, literally. After a few minutes, without the squats, I handed my answers to Wanda.

"So let's start on the left," she began." T-Bone you moved the fruit punch, lemonade, fruit cookies, fruit snacks and granola bars forward and you left the rest behind."

"Correct," he said.

"T-Bone, you got five wrong," she announced.

"I knew it," he grimaced. "I knew it. The soda's probably healthy."

"And Nicky," she continued, "your only change is that you would have left the fruit cookies behind."

"True," I said. "I mean, they're still cookies. I doubt fruit makes a cookie healthy."

"But it says they're made with fruit, Nick," said T-Bone, defending his decision. "*Fruit is healthy.*"

"Well, I'll give you the good news first," she said. "You made the same choices most people make."

"See, Nick, we're just like geniuses," T-Bone stated proudly. "Want me to guess the prices now? I used to watch *The Price is Right* all of the time."

"And the bad news is," she said, ignoring T-Bone, "you got a lot wrong."

"Hold on," said T-Bone, reversing the order of each item. "Now, they must be all correct."

"Still wrong," she laughed.

"How can they be wrong?" he wondered, while starting to do lunges across the kitchen.

"The question is: how can they be healthy?" she said with a smirk. "They're all unhealthy."

"Time out," I said. "They're all unhealthy? Every single one? Even the granola bar?"

"Yes, that bar isn't healthy," she confirmed.

"But it's a granola bar and doesn't granola mean healthy?" I persisted.

"No," she shook her head, "I'm pretty sure that's not the *definition of granola.*"

"What about fruit snacks and fruit punch?" asked T-Bone. "They're just like fruit. I see apples, grapes and pineapples. What's healthier than a fruit snack made of apples, grapes and pineapples?"

"I don't know," she answered, "*maybe fruit.*"

"But fruit snacks and fruit juice are just like fruit," T-Bone insisted. "Just chewier and wetter."

"No, they're not just like fruit," she explained. "They're mostly fruit flavors."

"Aren't they healthy flavors?" wondered T-Bone. "It's gotta be a lot healthier than chocolate."

Like a college professor, Wanda started explaining why each item was bad. She told us that the drinks were high in sugar as well as artificial colors and chemicals. The cookies, *even the fruit ones*, were high in sugar and fat, the chips had a lot of fat, and the granola bar had a lot of sugar. The fruit snacks that T-Bone insisted were healthy had lots of sugar and colors, but, ironically, very little fruit.

"You haven't mentioned teeth," T-Bone wondered. "Are these foods still bad for your teeth, or have they improved them?"

"How do you suppose they make sugar, artificial colors, and chemicals good for your teeth?" Wanda glared at T-Bone.

"More chemicals?" he asked with a shrug.

"Actually," she began, "not to get too far off topic, but since we're talking about teeth, you know that oral health affects your whole body, right?"

"Who's Oral?" asked T-Bone. "And why does his health affect me?"

"Oral means your mouth and your teeth," I said, shaking my head. "But I thought poor health could ruin your teeth."

"It can, but poor oral health can have serious side effects, too" she said. "And, it's really unnecessary."

"How can you stop it?" asked T-Bone. "When I was little, I remember having five cavities in one visit!"

"Five?" I gasped. "What did you do, sleep with a dozen lollipops in your mouth?"

"No, that would be dangerous," he replied. "I think the dentist told my mom that I ate too many fruit snacks and drank too much juice."

While T-Bone told us all about his dental dilemma, Wanda started Googling oral health. She went to the CDC's website for Children's Oral Health. It turned out that cavities, which are also called tooth decay, affected one in five children. It also said tooth decay is preventable. That was good news, because my mom always told us toothaches and earaches were awful. She said they were the worst.

"Uh-oh," Wanda said slowly. "This isn't good."

"It isn't preventable, after all?" I asked.
"Oh, no," she said, shaking her head, "it's definitely preventable, but the percentage of tooth decay for children in low-income families is twice as high as children from higher-income families."

"Seriously?" I asked. "That's so unfair, but why?"

"Well, some kids may live in areas that don't have fluoride in their water, they may not have money to get dental check-ups, they may not have enough money for toothpaste, or they may not know they should brush twice a day," she explained.

"Wow, twice as many is a lot," I said. "Do you think it's also related to the food? Remember, it's much harder for low-income families to buy healthy food."

"Definitely," she nodded. "That's a huge reason."

"Hold on," said T-Bone. "If we help people eat healthier, we'll be helping their teeth, which will help their health, which will help their teeth,..."

"Yes," Wanda cut him off. "Yes, that's exactly it. There are lots of reasons to make healthy choices."

"So, none of these would be a healthy choice?" I asked, pointing to the food display and still kind of shocked about the granola bar.

"No," Wanda said as she sensed my confusion and grabbed the box. "You know how you know?"

"You find a really smart friend, named Wanda, and you ask her?" T-Bone suggested.

"No," I said. "I think the answer she's looking for is: *read the nutritional label on the package.*"

"Exactly," said Wanda. "Go ahead."

"Go ahead what?" I asked.

She slid the box down the table. Unfortunately, she didn't know her own strength and she slid it a little harder than necessary. It whizzed by me and landed on the floor. I picked it up and examined the label. I knew about nutrition labels, but I'd never studied one. After a few seconds, I realized why. It was like reading in another language. Sure, I knew the words on the left: calories, fat, carbohydrates, sugar, protein, fiber, and sodium. But the measurements were confusing.

"Go ahead and read the label," she said.

"Just read it out loud?" I asked.

"Yup, read it and then decide if it's healthy," she said. "The nutritional information's right there."

"Let me see that," said T-Bone as he grabbed the box from my hands. "Oh, okay, there it is. I get it."

"What do you get?" asked Wanda.

"I've got all of the facts," he said. "See, right here, it has 100 calories, 3 gigabytes of fat, 7 gigabytes of sugar, and 75 megabytes of sodium."

"*Gigabytes?*" I laughed. "They don't use gigabytes and megabytes to measure nutrition, they use those for computers."

"T-Bone, they're actually grams and milligrams," said Wanda. "They're part of the metric system."

"Who uses that?" he asked.

"A lot of countries," she said, "but not the United States of America."

"Are you talking about centimeters and stuff like that?" he asked.

"Yes, like centimeters and liters," she explained. "But there's a huge problem."

"They're hard to spell?" said T-Bone.

"No, they're really hard to understand," said Wanda, "because we don't use the metric system."

"Hmmm," I nodded. "I never thought about it. I never really paid attention to these labels, but it's a lot like reading a foreign language. I know about teaspoons and tablespoons, but I couldn't tell you what 75 milligrams of sodium looks like."

"Oh, that's easy," said T-Bone. "It would look like 75 milligrams of salt because sodium is salt."

"I know that," I said. "I meant I don't know what *75 milligrams of anything* is equal to. Is it the size of the top of a pin, an eraser, or a small car? And, I don't know if any of those amounts are good."

"That's a big problem," Wanda agreed. "They keep adding more information to help us make good choices. Sadly, it doesn't help anyone to put all of the numbers on the label if no one knows what they mean. They may as well be in French, or Japanese, or...well, you know what I mean."

I grabbed the fruit punch and scanned the back nutrition label. It was a twenty-ounce bottle and the punch was bright red. I wondered why the size was the customary measurement of ounces and the rest was all metric. That didn't make any sense at all. It was like someone really didn't want us to know. I ran my finger down the label and stopped at the sugar.

"Wow! This one bottle has 71 grams of sugar," I announced. "Again, I don't know what a gram looks like, but 71 grams sounds like a lot."

Wanda pulled out her tablet and searched for a conversion of grams to something we could more easily understand, like teaspoons. When the answer appeared, she placed it in front of me.

"Holy moly," I gasped. "T-Bone, do you know how many teaspoons of sugar are in this bottle?"

"Well, my dad uses two teaspoons of sugar in his coffee and that bottle is a little bigger, so I'll guess three, maybe three and a half."

"Over 14 teaspoons," I said. "Over 14 teaspoons! I'm no doctor, but that sounds scary crazy."

"Are you sure?" asked T-Bone. "You should double

check. My mom gives me this fruit punch all of the time. She also hides the candy so I don't eat too much sugar."

"I used a gram-to-teaspoon converter, T-Bone," said Wanda. "It's correct."

"Is it less bad if you drink the sugar than if you eat the sugar, since you know, it's all wet?" he asked.

"Why would that matter?" I asked. "I'm sure wet sugar is the same as dry sugar."

"It is," Wanda laughed. "And do you know what's even funnier? You would eat less sugar with a chocolate candy bar."

"So you're saying that a delicious milk chocolate candy bar is healthier?" asked T-Bone.

"No," said Wanda, "I'm not saying it's healthier, I'm saying it has less sugar than the fruit punch."

"Hold on," I demanded. "Look at the ingredients. There are so many of them. You'd have to be a chemistry professor to understand this. Why do they make them sound like chemicals?"

"Because so many of them are chemicals," said

Wanda. "Why do you think it's so red? And why do you think it can sit on a shelf for so long without being refrigerated?"

"So if I drink that fruit punch, I'm drinking a lot of sugar mixed with chemicals?" I asked.

"What are we talking about?" asked my mom as she walked in. "And where did all of this junk food come from?"

"It's Wanda's," said T-Bone. "She brought it."

"We were just talking about sugar and chemicals in food," I answered.

"We aren't eating this," said Wanda. "It's part of our research."

"Oh, I see," said my mom. "Is this a school project?"

"Our next Garden State Adventure is going to bring New Jersey's kids to Healthytown on the Road to Wellness," exclaimed T-Bone.

"What's he talking about?" asked my mom, looking directly at me.

"After Dad's news, we decided to learn more about

diabetes and that led us to nutrition and wellness," I explained. "So our focus is on being healthy."

"Wow," my mom said with a smile. "I really love that you're focusing on wellness and health instead of diabetes. Even though it'll be manageable, it's still a change and I think change is always easier when you focus on the positives."

"That's what Mrs. Leary said," I agreed.

"Why did you go see Mrs. Leary?" my mom asked, running over to feel my forehead. "Nicky, are you not feeling well?"

Oh no, I thought. I should have never volunteered that information. I had to be very careful how I answered the question. If she knew I lied to see the nurse, she might be mad. If I said I didn't feel good, I might find myself in my room for days. My mom was the *Queen of the Quarantine*. This woman was no joke. She prided herself on outwitting viruses and infections. As soon as someone coughed or sniffed, they were quarantined in their room and then the disinfecting began. While the service was great, no one enjoyed the isolation.

"I, uh, had a stomach ache, I mean I had a small non-contagious, non-viral headache," I stumbled on each word. "Yes, that's what it was, a headache. Definitely a headache."

"Well, did you have any other symptoms at all? Congestion? Fever? Cough? Aches? Pains? Chills?" she quizzed me like the narrator on a cough syrup commercial. "You know what, stay here and I'll get the digital thermometer. If you have even a smidge of a temperature, you'll need to stay in your room."

"I lied," I blurted out. "Nothing was wrong. I just wanted to ask Mrs. Leary a few questions about diabetes. You don't have to quarantine curiosity."

"It's true, Mrs. A.," T-Bone confirmed. "I saw him leaving the nurse's office when I was going there."

"What?" she shrieked. "Are you not feeling well?"

"No, the good news," he said, "is that I'm fit as a fiddle. I was gonna fake being sick, too, but Nick beat me to it."

"Yeah, that's great news," she said with a hint of sarcasm. "Let me guess, Wanda, did you make a fake trip to the nurse, too?"

"Nope," she smiled and shook her head. "I handle all of my own research."

"Listen, boys, you didn't need to pretend you were sick to talk to the nurse," said my mom as she turned toward us.

"Well, if it makes you feel any better, I didn't do it very well," I said. "She saw right through me."

"I don't want you kids to worry about this," said my mom. "Your father and I will handle it. You should just focus on your schoolwork, being junior ambassadors, and basically trying to solve all of the world's problems."

"Mrs. A., with all due respect, you have access to three of the greatest research minds in the world," said T-Bone. "Well, technically, that's Wanda. We're kinda like backup singers. But we're all ready to find out what we need to do to keep Mr. A. healthy. Plus, we're family."

"I suppose by now we are," my mom said with a smile. "So what did we find out? Truth be told, I was planning to do my own research, but I haven't had a second to get started."

We gave my mom Wanda's healthy food/unhealthy food test and she also failed. Ironically, she did know the price of every item, right down to the penny, and she even had coupons for three of them.

She told us she has been reading labels for years and never gave much thought to the use of metric measurements. While she did know what the abbreviations stood for, she admitted that she only really understood calories. It turns out that was more than we even understood. She suggested we use sugar cubes to convert sugar grams. Since each cube was one teaspoon, it would be a great way to actually see how much sugar was in different foods. One thing was clear, learning how to eat healthy was more challenging than we thought.

"Mrs. A., do you mind if I look in your pantry?" asked Wanda.

"Sure, sweetie," said my mom, more than happy to show off her super-organized pantry.

"Wow, this is super organized," said Wanda. *This girl always knew the right thing to say.*

While we were looking at labels on the unhealthy buffet, Wanda emerged, carrying a variety of different items. She then grabbed her tablet and pulled up an app called Fooducate.

"Why are you taking pictures of our food?" Timmy asked, as he walked in with his friend, Wyatt, right behind him.

"I'm not taking pictures," she explained without looking up. "I'm scanning the bar codes."

"Okay," he replied. "Why are you doing that?"
"Because," she began, "I found this great app called Fooducate that gives food grades based upon their nutritional value. It also tells you why the foods earned those grades and gives alternatives."

"Did the food study?" Wyatt giggled. "Or did you find a *bad apple*?"

We all stopped what we were doing and looked at each other. Well, everyone except T-Bone. It was shocking. Timmy's new friend instantly reminded everyone of a younger T-Bone. If T-Bone wasn't the youngest kid in his family, I would have bet that he was T-Bone's little brother. Wyatt had only been to our house a few times and I always knew he reminded me of someone. Now, I knew who it was; *it was T-Bone*. He was just a smaller version. I couldn't wait until my dad got to know him.

"Maybe the foods that received A's studied," said Wanda, "but I know one thing, based upon its grade, chocolate syrup didn't do much studying."

"Maybe it needs a food tutor," said Wyatt. "We could call it a *futor*. Get it, Mrs. A.?"

My mom stared at him, wide-eyed, wondering how both of her sons could be friends with, basically, the same kid just in different sized clothes.

"Mrs. A., where do you keep your measuring spoons and measuring cups?" asked Wanda.

"Top drawer near the stove," my mom answered.

Wanda grabbed a tablespoon and held up the chocolate syrup. "The serving size for this syrup is two tablespoons," she began. "Now, everything on the label is based upon just two tablespoons."

"Hold on," Wyatt interrupted. "That's not right. When I make myself chocolate milk, I probably use about six of those big spoons, unless my mom isn't looking. Then I would use about eight or twelve."

"First," said Wanda, "ew, that's way too much."

"No such thing as too much chocolate," said Wyatt, suddenly reminding me of Maggie.

"Actually," said my mom, "there is definitely a thing called too much chocolate. And, you raised a great point, Wanda. Most people don't know what the serving size really is when reading labels."

"What do you mean?" I asked. "Doesn't the serving size just mean the amount you use?"

"Think about it," my mom explained. "If a food has 300 calories for a ½ cup portion and you have 2 cups, you would have to multiply every number on that label by four. Since everyone uses different amounts, the serving size on a label could never just be the amount you use."

"I never thought about that," I admitted. "I guess I figured whatever amount I eat is the serving size. Now that you bring it up, I suppose the numbers can't be the same for all different sizes."

"But the serving sizes must be pretty close to what most people would eat?" asked T-Bone. "Right?"

"I can answer that," my mom laughed. "No, sometimes they aren't close at all. I can tell you from years of trying different diets and also counting calories, some serving sizes are ridiculously small. You know those big bowls you kids use for cereal? Fill it up and it can easily be four servings. That means every number must be multiplied by four."

"Why would they make the serving size so small?" I asked. "It almost sounds like the food companies want to make it confusing on purpose. Why don't they make the size what real people actually eat?"

"Not all of them, but many companies do try to confuse consumers," said Wanda, holding up the tablespoon again. "Look at this bottle of French salad dressing. The serving size is two of these."

"I use way more than that," said T-Bone. "I like to soak my salad."

"Most people do," said Wanda. "But each serving of two tablespoons has 120 calories. If you used four tablespoons, that would be 240 calories. If you have a big salad and you use six tablespoons, that's 360 calories *just on the salad dressing.*"

"You know, Wanda," said my mom, "I just read an article in a magazine that discussed how people think all salads are healthy. But, sometimes, a salad has more calories than steak and a potato."

"Let's see," said T-Bone, "when my mom makes a salad she puts cheddar cheese, onions, carrots, bacon bits, croutons, and sometimes eggs on top. I don't think it can be bad if it's on lettuce. I think lettuce has some sort of secret powers. Wait — that's probably the reason Mr. A. loves fruits and vegetables so much. Maybe your dad is a super-hero and we don't know it."

"What?" I laughed. "Now, you think my dad might be a superhero?"

"Maybe," said T-Bone. "Superheroes always keep their identities hidden. And, that's probably why there are so many kinds of salads; lettuce must have special powers."

"Ha!" my mom exclaimed. "First of all, Mr. A. is a good guy, but he's not a superhero. And yes, lettuce is healthy, but have you ever seen a Chef's Salad?"

"Not really," said T-Bone. "I don't know any chefs well enough to get that close to their plates."

"Not a salad that belongs to a particular chef," Wanda corrected. "My mom orders Chef's Salads sometimes. I think it's lettuce, tomato, cheese, ham, turkey, egg, and croutons. Oh, and dressing."

"Think about it," said my mom. "What's the real difference between that salad and a hoagie? They both have cheese, meats, lettuce, tomato, and bread. The Chef's Salad isn't served on bread, but the croutons are just cut up bread. And, of course, the salad also has dressing and egg."

"But it's on lettuce," insisted T-Bone. "Therefore, it must be good for you."

"You know, back in the old days, salad was mostly lettuce, tomato, cucumber, onion, and maybe some other vegetables," said my mom. "Now, it can be a whole order of chicken tenders with cheese, bacon, egg, croutons, and salad dressing. *A salad is only as healthy as what's in it.*"

"So, you're saying it really depends on what you put on the salad?" asked T-Bone. "But the lettuce is still healthy, right?"

"Yes and yes," my mom laughed.

"How about jelly beans on lettuce?" asked Wyatt.

"I was just thinking the same exact thing," T-Bone exclaimed, high-fiving Wyatt.

Wow, he really was just a smaller, younger T-Bone. I couldn't wait for my dad to really get to know this kid. I decided not to warn him, I figured it would make a much better surprise. I just hoped I could be there when he figured it out.

For the next two hours, we scanned almost every item in the pantry. Most of the food grades were surprising. Unfortunately, they weren't good surprises. Especially when we looked at the real serving sizes. It seemed like a dirty trick. Some foods that came in small bags had a serving size of half of the bag. The bags were so small, I couldn't imagine why they didn't just make one bag the serving size and then double the numbers. Wanda insisted that they did it to keep the numbers low and they assumed that most people who actually looked at the calories would figure the whole bag was the serving.

It was amazing. I had been eating food my whole life and I apparently knew nothing about it. In just a few hours I learned that serving sizes are tricky, measurements are in a different language, putting something on lettuce doesn't automatically make it healthy, two tablespoons are pretty small, *and Wyatt was the younger brother T-Bone always wanted.*

Chapter Three

A T-Bone and a Half

By the time my dad came home, we had put most of the kitchen put back together. That is, except for the foods my mom was removing.

"Hi, honey," he said as he walked into the kitchen with a big bag of groceries.

"Hi, Mr. A.," T-Bone answered. "Bad news. I see that lettuce sticking out of your shopping bag."

"And?" asked my dad.

"You should know that it doesn't have nutritional super powers," he explained. "Romaine lettuce is nutritional, but it still doesn't have powers."

"Thanks for the heads-up," he said as he placed the bag on the counter. "It's weird, I kept waiting for it to fly around the house and...nothing. Now, I know why; no special powers."

Luckily, T-Bone never got my dad's sarcasm. Wanda and I, on the other hand, always got it.

"Hon, the kids have been doing some research about diabetes, nutrition, and wellness in general," my mom told my dad.

"Really?" he nodded and smiled, a little surprised. "Thanks, guys."

"And FYI, a jelly bean salad is not good for you."

"Got it, T-Bone," my dad said, without turning around. "I'm sure that'll come in handy one..."

"I'm not T-Bone, Mr. A., I'm Wyatt," a small voice interrupted.

My dad slowly turned around, stared at Wyatt, looked at T-Bone and then looked back at Wyatt. Then he did it again and scratched his head.

"Sorry about that," my dad shrugged. "Boy, he reminds me of someone. I just can't figure it out."

"I'm sure it'll come to you," said my mom.

While my mom unloaded the dishwasher, we showed our research to my dad. He was impressed, even with T-Bone. Of course it helped that Wanda never took the credit for herself. She never said "I found this" or "I did that"; *it was always we.*

While everyone discussed things like cucumbers and potato chips, I walked into the pantry to put the last few cans away. My mom was sitting on a stool with her head on her lap. She never heard me walk in and when she looked up, I froze.

"Hey, Mom, are you okay?" I asked.

"Oh, Nicky, yes, I'm sorry. Yes, I'm fine," she said as she jumped up, wiping her eyes.

"You don't look fine," I said. "Are you nervous about Dad?"

"No, no, not at all," she said with a forced smile. "No, this will all be fine."

"Why does it look like you were crying?" I asked.

"No, no, don't be silly," she fake laughed, "I wasn't crying, it's my allergies. It's all of this stupid dust."

"Uh huh," I nodded, totally unconvinced. "If I had to guess, I would say you're upset because you either realized the majority of the food industry has been kind of deceiving us or you're really afraid that Dad's diabetes is worse than you're letting on. Or, there's a third choice...you just realized Timmy's BFF is an exact, but smaller, duplicate of T-Bone. Am I getting warmer?"

She actually laughed for a moment, grabbed a roll of paper towels, and started blowing her nose and wiping her eyes.

"I'm not upset," she insisted. "Just overwhelmed. I'm overwhelmed at school with the ridiculous amounts of nonsensical paperwork and reports that really don't help my students. I'm frustrated with the constant testing. And, because of all that, I haven't had time to prepare the kinds of meals I used to make for my own family."

"Mom, you don't really think you gave dad diabetes because you've been making some quick meals and serving some take-out, do you?"

"I don't know," she shrugged. "It can't be helping. Plus, I've been standing in here for ten minutes and I can't think of anything to make for dinner. Every time I get an idea, I look at the label. How can I keep your father and you kids healthy for a lifetime when I can't think of anything to make for dinner right now?"

Oh, no, I thought. She really was upset. I couldn't think of anything to say and started wishing I'd sent Wanda into the pantry to put those cans away. She would have known exactly what to say. Then it occurred to me. I simply needed to think like Wanda. What would she say, I thought to myself. What would she say?

"Mom, I think everyone is overwhelmed," I said, feeling like that was a good Wanda-start. "But I don't think anyone expects you to have all of the answers so fast, or even ever."

She bit her lower lip, looked up and half-smiled. Unfortunately, she still didn't know what she was going to make for dinner. While I put the last cans back on the shelf, I heard T-Bone yell, "Eureka!" My mom and I looked at each and shook our heads.

"Nick, Nick, wait until you see what Wanda just stumbled upon," he exclaimed. "The American Diabetes Association has a huge website and it has so many cool things like living with diabetes and food and fitness. It even has a meal planner."

My mom and I both jumped up. Leave it to T-Bone to solve a problem he didn't even know existed.

"You know what, Nick?" she whispered. "Maybe this will be okay."

"I know," I agreed. "Who knows, maybe it's not the lettuce with super powers, maybe it's the T-Bone."

With a newly dried off face and an actual smile, my mom looked over Wanda's shoulder to see the site.

"Mrs. A.," said Wanda as she realized my mom was back, "if you haven't already planned tonight's dinner, we could we try the meal planner."

"Well, I always have something planned," she said as she winked at me, "but this sounds like fun. Let's try this instead. How does it work?"

While they explored the www.diabetes.org website, I noticed my mom start to relax a little bit. The website was filled with information; they had thought of everything you would need to know to live with diabetes.

About half an hour later, my mom and Wanda had dinner under control and were picking out recipes for the rest of the week. With so much activity, my dad actually invited T-Bone and Wanda to stay for dinner. Too bad he didn't realize Wyatt and Timmy were right behind him.

"Dinner sounds great," said Wyatt. "I'm sure my mom won't mind."

My dad looked at my mom and, once again, told her that Wyatt really reminded him of someone; he just couldn't think of whom. Interestingly, T-Bone didn't notice any similarities, either. In fact, when Wyatt inadvertently accepted my dad's invitation, T-Bone seemed a little shocked.

"Boy, this kid's not shy about accepting invitations, is he?" T-Bone commented and shook his head.

My mom and Wanda prepared a big, healthy salad with cucumbers, peppers, apple slices, and carrots while my dad grilled some chicken. Much to Wyatt's disappointment, there were no jelly beans on the salad; not even fruit-flavored. When the salad was completed, my mom made some brown rice that boiled right in its own little bags and steamed some broccoli. The whole time she cooked, she seemed relaxed. I wasn't sure if it was having Wanda give her a hand or if it was feeling like she wasn't alone in making these food choices. Before my dad's visit to the doctor, I doubt my mom ever thought all that much about the meals she made. While she wasn't serving ice cream sundaes for breakfast and cake for lunch, I think she always assumed she was making healthy choices. And no one could blame her because who would have ever guessed how much sugar and how many chemicals were added to our foods?

Even though nothing exciting happened, that dinner was one I would probably remember for the rest of my life. It was the exact night we all started looking at food differently. We were now curious about the ingredients and learning about sensible portions. It was also the most squished I ever was at the dinner table. Besides the six people in my family, we squeezed in Wanda, T-Bone, and even Wyatt. While our chicken wasn't deep fried or covered with cheese- and even with a T-Bone and a half at the table- my dad seemed really happy.

Later that night, Pop stopped by.

"Hey, Pop, what are you doing here?" I asked.

"I was visiting a buddy of mine who lives nearby and I thought I'd stop over," he explained.

"Hi, Pop," said Wyatt as he walked by him. "What's shakin', crispy bacon?"

My grandfather did a double take and then asked who the kid was. When we told him, he paused. He looked around and asked if Wyatt reminded us of anyone in particular. My mom and I just laughed. My dad still couldn't put his finger on it.

"So what's new?" asked Pop.

"Well, we're becoming experts in nutrition," I said with undue authority.

"And exercise," T-Bone added as he suddenly started jogging in place.

"You don't say," Pop observed. "Does this have any-thing to do with my son?"

"Actually, everything," I admitted.

"Then this is a good thing," Pop nodded.

"How is this a good thing?" asked T-Bone. "Last week Mr. A. was healthy and now he has diabetes. How can diabetes be healthy?"

"Very simple," said Pop. "Last week no one was paying attention to food and nutrition. Now, Nick's whole family, you, Wanda, and even the little version of you will pay attention to what you eat."

"*Little version of me?*" asked T-Bone, completely oblivious to the similarities.

"Anyway," Pop continued, ignoring T-Bone, "my son will eat all of the right things and he'll be fine. And you guys will have enough knowledge to make good, healthy decisions about what you eat."

"Oh, I get it," said T-Bone, "this way if we end up getting diabetes, we'll be ready."

"No, no," Pop laughed. "If you learn how to eat well at your age, you might actually avoid things like diabetes, obesity, high blood pressure, and heart disease in the future."

"Hold on! You can try to avoid those things?" asked T-Bone. "No way! Do you take a pill?"

"If you make great choices, you may not need any pills when you grow up," Pop said with a smile.

"Is there a mist for your nose?" asked T-Bone. "Just in case the healthy stuff doesn't work out."

"No, no, no," Pop answered. "No mist, no pills, just eating healthy and making smart choices."

"Staying healthy with food?" I asked. "Sounds kind

of far-fetched and impossible. Every three minutes there's a commercial on for some new medicine that to treat something. The only problem is, when they read the side effects, most sound worse than the original problem."

"Actually," Wanda piped up, "my grandmother says that our diet is the one factor, besides genes, that can keep us healthy, or at least healthier."

"She must be a smart lady," Pop agreed. "Did you know that my generation never had a lot of the illnesses and allergies young people have today? Now, I'm not a scientist, but I think many of these things are food-related."

"That doesn't make any sense to me," said Timmy. "How can it be different from when you were younger? Foods haven't changed."

"Oh, they sure have changed," said Pop. "For starters, we didn't have fast food or too much processed food. We mostly ate a lot of fruits and vegetables and people had time to cook real food."

"Oh, good news! You don't need a lot of time anymore," said T-Bone. "They have whole meals you can microwave in two minutes."

"That's what I'm talking about," said Pop. "Ever read the labels on frozen meals and boxed meals?"

"My grandmother says you have to be a scientist to figure out what's in food," Wanda agreed. "She also said some ingredients, like sugar, have many names. Nana said there are over forty names for sugar, including corn syrup, high-fructose corn syrup, dextrose, brown sugar, caramel, dextran, glucose, malt syrup, maltose, and sucrose."

"Wow, you really did your homework," said Pop. "And, so did your Nana."

"Thanks," Wanda smiled. "She also said processed foods have artificial colors and sweeteners and there are lots of questions about their safety. She even said some chemicals that our country allows are banned in other countries."

"What?" T-Bone gasped. "How can that be?"

"That's scary," I said. "Eating healthy foods will be harder than we thought. How can people really make sure their foods are healthy?"

"You have to know where to look," Pop said with a smile. "Do you kids know where the healthiest foods in the grocery store are located?"

"In the front," guessed Timmy.

"Nope," Pop laughed.

"Oh, in the back," said T-Bone.

"Nope."

"I give up," said Timmy.

"Around the edge of the store," said Pop. "It's called the perimeter and it's along the walls."

We tried to picture the grocery store aisles. I went shopping with my dad and his coupons weekly and now I couldn't remember where anything other than the cereal aisle was. We all looked confused; *except for Wanda, of course.*

"You mean the dairy, meats, fruits and vegetables, right?" she asked.

"Yup," said Pop. "That's where you find whole foods."

"Like donuts and Swiss cheese?" asked Wyatt.

"Correct," said T-Bone.

"Incorrect, they don't mean foods with holes,"

Wanda asserted. "I think he means foods that don't come from food factories. Those are the foods that either haven't been processed or have been minimally processed."

"Pardon me, Madame President, but foods aren't made in factories," said T-Bone. "Shoes are made in factories. Cars are made in factories. I'm pretty sure bikes are made in factories. But foods aren't."

"First of all," she began, "I told you not to call me Madame President. Second, foods certainly are made in factories. They're called processed foods."

"She's right," Pop nodded.

"I don't believe it," T-Bone protested. "Are you trying to tell me that they make cookies in the same factories where they make cars?"

"That's dumb," said Wyatt. "Everybody knows some elves make cookies in trees. And on the orange juice commercial, they squeeze the whole orange through the top of the bottle. No factories there."

"Wow, you guys have your work cut out for you," Pop said as he looked at me and Wanda. "But this is a good conversation. It tells us something."

"What could these guys believing cookies are made by elves and orange juice comes from squeezing a whole orange into a bottle tell us?" I wondered.

"Consider them your sample group," said Pop. "Other kids could be thinking the same things."

"I never thought about it that way," I admitted. "But they're kind of a small, goofy sample."

"Did you hear that, boys?" T-Bone said with a big smile. *"We're samples."*

"Is that good?" asked Timmy.

"Are you kidding?" said T-Bone. "Everyone loves free samples."

"Hold on," said Wanda. "That gives me an idea. Pop's right, I bet most people don't understand these things. Let's make it a school initiative. As the co-presidents, we want to make sure everyone is healthy, and at least knows how to be healthy."

"Go on," said T-Bone. "I don't know where you're going with this, but I like it."

"Let's do a questionnaire," she began, "to find out what kids really know and get a bigger sample."

"So we won't be the only samples?" asked Wyatt.

"You'll still be samples," said Wanda. "Now, you'll just be part of a bigger group of samples."

"That's a good idea," I agreed. "But then what? What happens when we find out what we already suspect; that everyone is confused."

"Then we address it," she responded with her usual confidence. "This is perfect. The questions will tell us what confuses people most and then we can explain those things. Maybe we could even have demonstrations at school."

"Now, you're talking," said T-Bone. "Let's protest!"

"Not that kind of a demonstration," I said as I shook my head. "Like a food demonstration."

"Ooh, ooh, I'll be the chef," T-Bone volunteered. "Remember, I did bake with the Cake Boss! I'll bring a whisk. And a spare whisk, just in case."

"I don't think they'll let us cook at school," Wanda laughed. "I was thinking of showing kids some of the issues raised in the questionnaires."

"What issues?" asked Timmy.

"That all depends on their answers," I said.

"You may want to include advice for selecting whole foods," warned Pop.

"Why?" I wondered. "Aren't they the good foods?"

"Yes, but they have issues, too," he explained. "If the produce isn't certified organic, it was probably treated with pesticides."

"That's funny," I laughed. "I almost thought you meant poisons on our foods."

"I did," Pop nodded. "They're chemicals used to keep pests away from crops and the reason you should always thoroughly wash your fruits and vegetables before you eat them."

"That's kinda scary," said T-Bone. "Is that the only whole food warning?"

"Actually," he continued, "consumers must be very savvy when shopping. Many farm animals are given things like steroids and hormones to improve their size and health."

"That doesn't sound bad," said T-Bone. "I like to picture nice plump chickens running around the farm, playing with the ducks while spotted, hefty cows graze alongside horses and goats."

"You do paint a nice picture, but that's not exactly the scene at many factory farms," warned Pop. "Animals are often kept in small cages, packed in so tightly, they can't move. At some factory farms, the conditions can be horrific."

"What?" T-Bone exclaimed. "How can that be?"

"Even worse, whatever they give those animals to eat goes into the milk, meat, and eggs," said Pop.

"This is terrible," I said. "What about the free range chickens? I've seen packages that say free range. Are they the happy little chickens that get to run around and frolic with each other?"

"Hardly," said Pop. "There's a difference between what people believe terms like *free range* and *cage free* mean, and what they actually mean. Sometimes, instead of cages, they're crammed in sheds."

"What's the difference between being crammed in a cage or a shed?" I asked.

"Basically," Pop shrugged, "*a word*."

"Wow," I said, shaking my head. "This is getting more complicated by the minute. Hey, Pop, can you help us come up with some good questions?"

"Absolutely," he smiled. "Just remember, kids, even difficult, complicated situations can be solved once people understand everything about them. Be careful, though, to check your sources. Never use just one source. And, check for motive."

"Motive?" I asked.

"Sure," he replied. "You can read an article and think you know everything about a topic and then you notice who wrote the article."

"And?" asked T-Bone.

"And then you see that every fact and statistic was carefully selected to support one side of the issue," he explained. "Depending upon motivation, you may only be getting one side of the story. That's why you should always use multiple sources."

"I feel like you almost have to be a detective just to make a healthy breakfast," I said.

"Nope," Pop laughed, "you have to be a detective to make a healthy *breakfast, lunch, and dinner*."

Chapter Four

Too Young To Retire

The rest of that night we made a list of questions. Working as a group, and working in the kitchen, made it fun. My parents joined us and soon we had over fifty good questions. From *Which food has more sugar?* to *How many teaspoons of sugar are in the following foods?* From *How big is a serving of cereal?* to *What's the difference between white and wheat bread?* Coming up with questions was easier than we thought it would be, mostly because we knew way less than we thought we knew.

The next day at lunch, Wanda handed me a two-page questionnaire. This girl really was amazing. She took all of the notes from the night before and created a professional-looking document. It looked so good that, at first, I thought it was something she just downloaded and printed. Once I skimmed through it, I realized they were our questions.

"So what's the next step?" asked T-Bone.

"I already spoke to Ms. Swanson and she said we can pass them out tomorrow morning during first period," said Wanda.

"Good job, Madame...never mind," T-Bone stopped himself. "I mean, Wanda."

"Thanks," she said as she packed up her tote bag and headed out of the cafeteria. "See you later."

"I think she loves me," T-Bone whispered.

"What on Earth makes you think that?" I asked.

"She didn't roll her eyes and she also said thanks," he explained.

"She was just being polite," I said as I rolled my own eyes. "Trust me, T, she's not in love with you."

"It's okay if you don't believe it right now," he said. "You'll believe it when you're at our wedding."

That was the thing about T-Bone; he was the most hopeful, optimistic person I had ever met. I don't even think poor Wanda knew what she was up against. I just hoped he didn't eventually scare her away. In the beginning, I was definitely not a big Wanda fan and I definitely didn't want her to be T-Bone's Co-President or the third Unofficial Junior Ambassador. However, once we worked together, I surprised myself. I started to appreciate how smart and organized she was. She really kept us focused and she was an amazing researcher. The best part, however, was that as hard as T-Bone tried, she basically ignored him.

Shortly before last period, I heard Wanda and T-Bone called to the main office over the speaker. I just assumed it was student council business until T-Bone knocked on my classroom door. He told my teacher that my presence was requested. My teacher looked confused and just said, "Okay."

"Why couldn't you just say the office needs Nick Abruzzi?" I asked as we started down the hallway. "Why are you so dramatic? What's with the 'requests your presence thing'? This isn't the Royal Ball, you know."

"I don't know," he shrugged. "Personally, I think it sounded more presidential."

"Why am I being called to the office?" I asked.

"Ms. Swanson discussed our questionnaire with some teachers and they had an idea they wanted to run by us," he explained.

"Wow," I said. "The teachers have an idea for us?"

"Yeah, pretty cool, huh?" he nodded.

Ms. Swanson was the student council moderator and seemed to really respect T-Bone and Wanda. She recognized that they ran for office for the right reasons. They both wanted to become president to accomplish good things, not just for the title or to boss people around.

"Hi, guys," she said as we walked into her office. "Sorry to pull you from class, but I have some good news. I shared your questionnaire with some of the teachers and they were impressed; to be honest, they were impressed and excited."

"Thank you," said Wanda.

"I have to say," she continued, "you three kids are very ambitious. Between taking your stands for New Jersey, public schools, poverty, and literacy, I don't know where you find the time or the energy.

It's really admirable that you are now raising awareness for nutrition and wellness."

"Well, we had a good reason for this one," I said. "The doctor thinks my dad might have diabetes."

"Oh," she said as she abruptly stopped and looked at me. "That must've been a shock for your family."

"You ain't kidding," said T-Bone. "We were floored. He's a produce manager and a big fan of fruits and vegetables. I know I didn't see this coming."

"Wait," she hesitated, "this is *Nick's dad,* right?"

"Yup," T-Bone nodded again.

"T-Bone thinks he's part of my family," I laughed.

"Correction," he said holding up one finger, "I am part of the family. Except for sleeping hours, I'm probably at your house more than your dad."

"It's true," I told Ms. Swanson. "He is there a lot."

"Well, I think it's very generous of all of you to get involved," she continued. "And because diabetes, obesity, and heart disease are at epidemic levels, all of the teachers think this is a great initiative."

"Thank you," said Wanda. "We're excited to hear about their ideas."

"Well, we thought we should have a wellness fair," she began.

"No way! That's awesome!" exclaimed T-Bone. "I love fairs. We can have bounce houses, cotton candy, candy apples and snow cones. This'll be awesome, but the candy apples should be caramel, not the red hard stuff. They get messy fast, trust me. I once had that red stuff in my hair for days."

"Are you serious?" I asked, totally flabbergasted.

"Oh, alright, relax. We can have both kinds of candy apples," T-Bone conceded.

"No, Tommy," said Ms. Swanson, "He's referring to the fact that this would be a *wellness fair*."

"Uh huh," T-Bone nodded.

"And we should probably focus on healthy things," Wanda said very slowly, hoping he would get it.

"So just the caramel?" asked T-Bone.

"Maybe just the apples," I said, shaking my head.

"And, before you ask, no funnel cakes."

"Hmmm," he mumbled to himself, "doesn't sound like much of a fair."

"Actually, the fair would be the culminating activity for a program designed to teach everyone how to be healthy," said Ms. Swanson.

"So we would be doing things before the fair?" asked Wanda.

"Exactly," Ms. Swanson said with a big smile and paging through her notes. "Mrs. Leary and the gym teachers would like to contribute their skills. And my good friend, Dr. Lisa Seed, offered to share her insights. She's an amazing doctor and a mom."

"Wow, this is getting big," I said, suddenly feeling a little overwhelmed. I started thinking about our jobs as Unofficial Junior Ambassadors, our odd job business, *At Your Service*, our other causes, and of course, school. I wanted to help my dad be healthy, but I wondered, once again, how three kids could pull off something so big, again.

"I love the whole idea," said a very excited Wanda. "Imagine the impact. If we can influence several hundred kids and teachers who then bring that information home and tell others, we may be able to impact thousands of people."

"Thousands?" I asked, feeling my heart race.

"Nick, you don't look so good," said T-Bone. "Would you like some healthy water?"

"Yeah, what's wrong?" asked Wanda. "This is an incredible opportunity. What's the problem?"

"It just seems like a lot and...," I started to explain.

"Nicky," Ms. Swanson interrupted. "I don't want you to stress over this. Your simple questionnaire has not only inspired the teachers; we also want to do the work with you. I also presented it to the school administration as well and they're on board. Last I heard, the secretaries, the custodians, the cafeteria staff, and even the bus drivers will be involved."

"That fast?" I asked, still finding it hard to believe. "Well, not to brag," she said with a smile, "but one well-written e-mail to explain a very important initiative was all we needed. Now, we have an all-hands-on-deck situation. Isn't it just wonderful?"

Before I could even answer, I noticed T-Bone's foot

moving very close to me. He was suddenly in the middle of a lunge. I was hoping we could wrap it up before he started doing squats and jumping jacks. When he went into his third lunge, I knew there was no way she wouldn't notice. He was now on the other side of her office.

"Whatcha doin' there?" I asked in that scary parent voice with the scary parent smile, hoping he would stop before Ms. Swanson noticed.

"Multi-tasking," he said with a big grin.

"It's okay, Nicky," she said, sensing my discomfort. "Tommy's definitely, how should I say this, a little unorthodox, but maybe that's what we need."

"I guess," I said as I stood up to return to class. "Um, thank you, um, for helping us with this."

"Don't look so worried," she smiled. "Teachers are professionals. We've got this! Anyway, with all of this ridiculous testing and endless, meaningless paperwork, we would all love an opportunity to go back to actually teaching useful things creatively. Now, we have our chance."

After our meeting, my mind was a blur. I wasn't sure how we would pull this off, but with dozens of teachers and staff, as well as Wanda, we were probably in good hands. Plus, we had pulled off some other great ideas, like CODE READ, where we gave away thousands of books to kids in the City of Trenton. That one made me really nervous, too, but as usual, Wanda, T-Bone, and an army of volunteers stepped up to help.

By the time we left Ms. Swanson's office, it was time to pack up for the bus. As usual, I knew T-Bone and Wanda were coming over. And as usual, T-Bone stopped at his house first. Once again, even with running to his house, he still almost beat me home. Maybe he had super powers, I thought. When he walked in, I could smell his dad's aftershave, stronger than usual. That just meant he was really trying to impress Wanda. Sadly, the more he put on, the farther Wanda sat from him. It was so strong today, I wouldn't have been surprised if she sat across the street.

"So, what should we do first?" he asked.

"Wait for Wanda," I answered. "Definitely wait."

"Good point," he agreed as he popped his head out the front door.

"Relax, I'm sure she'll be here soon," I laughed.

"I know," he nodded, "I just don't want my dad's aftershave to wear off before she gets here."

"T-Bone, she could arrive in thirty-seven-years and she'd still smell you from around the block."

"You sure?" he asked. "Because it guarantees it'll drive that special someone crazy. But in order to work, she has to smell it."

"Oh, she'll smell it," I said with my most dramatic nod. "She'll definitely smell it."

"Wow, what's that awful smell?" my dad asked as he walked in from the kitchen. "Did a garbage truck full of skunks break down out front?"

"Good one, Mr. A.," said T-Bone. "But don't worry, there's no garbage truck full of skunks; it's just me and my dad's aftershave."

"Sure you grabbed the right bottle?" asked my dad.

"Sure did," T-Bone responded. "I'm just relieved you can still smell it. I was afraid it wore off."

"Wore off?" my dad laughed. "Kid, I could strap you to the top of my car, pay for the extra scrubbing, and drive you through the car wash 20 times and you still wouldn't have anything to worry about."

"Wow, that's saying something," T-Bone said with a smile. "Thanks, Mr. A."

"Hey, Dad, why are you home so early?" I asked.

"Let me guess," said T-Bone. "You were named Fruit and Vegetable Man of the Year and as your prize you get to go home early for the day?"

"No," my dad said as he shook his head. "I just got back from the doctor's office.

"What did she say?" I asked.

"Wait," T-Bone said as he covered his mouth. "You were at the doctor's office? What did she say?"

"Well," my dad began in a soft and calm voice, "we should wait for everyone else to get home."

"Oh no, I knew it. It's bad news," said T-Bone as he covered his mouth with his other hand. "I knew it was gonna be bad. Okay, Mr. A., listen to me, this'll be okay. You are not doomed. Do you hear me? You are not doomed."

"What are you doing?" I whispered. "Stop it!"

"It's okay, Nick," said my dad. "Not everybody can handle *no news* well."

"So, exactly what kind of news are we talking about?" I asked, hoping to trick him into talking.

"Nice try," my dad laughed. "But I think we'll just wait for everybody else."

No sooner had my dad said that, then my mom and my sisters walked in. A moment later, Timmy and Wyatt parked their bikes and came bouncing through the front door. My mom looked distracted-it was at that moment that I realized she also was expecting bad news.

"Okay, since everyone's here, even Tommy, I should tell you what the doctor said," he began. "Yes, I do have Type 2 diabetes. But it's not super bad. We're going to start treatment with diet and exercise first. I just have to make some changes."

"You mean, *we* need to make some changes," said T-Bone.

"I have a question," said Timmy. "What even is diabetes? On the commercials they always talk about high blood sugar, but then they say low blood sugar. Which one is it? Does it mean the sugar is confused? Because I'm confused."

"Actually," said my mom, "diabetes happens when someone's body can't use a sugar called glucose."

"That's okay," said Timmy. "Sugar's bad anyway."

"Well, that glucose is the main energy for the body's cells," she explained. "And you need a thing called insulin to control the amount of glucose."

"Okay," Timmy tried to keep up, "where does the insulin come from?"

"It's a hormone made in the pancreas," my mom continued. "You see, if your pancreas isn't making insulin, glucose doesn't enter your cells normally."

"My doctor told me that a good way to explain insulin is like this," said my dad. "Insulin works like a key to a door. Think of every cell in your body as having a locked door. Insulin is the key that unlocks the locks and opens the doors to the cells of your body. When the doors swing open, the sugar in your bloodstream can enter your cells, and your body uses that sugar for energy."

"Wow," my mom said with a smile. "That was a perfect definition for kids."

"She got it from the Diabetes Research Institute Foundation," said my dad. "It turns out there are a lot of great places to find answers online. So, we can relax. I'll listen to my doctor and be just fine."

As my dad finished speaking, Wanda knocked on the front door. It was a good diversion. My mom looked like she desperately wanted to talk to my dad without any kids listening.

"What's going on?" asked Wanda. "It feels very serious in this room. Is everything okay?"

"Now, it's time for Nick to worry," said T-Bone.

"What are you talking about?" I asked. "*Before* I was worried, when we didn't know what was gonna happen, and that's when you said 90% of what we worry about never even happens."

"Exactly," T-Bone confirmed. "But that was before the 10% just happened. Who knew your dad would be in the 10%?"

"But I honestly feel better right now," I said. "My dad was just diagnosed with Type 2 diabetes and I actually feel better."

"How can you possibly feel better?" asked T-Bone.

Then he leaned in and whispered, "Your father has diabetes."

"I know," I said. "I get it, but honestly, it's better than not knowing."

"You're crazy," he insisted. "When you don't know an answer yet, there's still a chance that you can get good news. Now that you know, that chance is gone. Evaporated. Disintegrated. Gone."

"You're wrong," Wanda said very casually. "Other than the fear of speaking in public, for most people there is no greater fear than fear of the unknown."

"Oh, really? How about spiders? Or snakes? Or the dark?" said T-Bone.

"No," Wanda replied. "The unknown is worse."

"I agree," I said. "Now that we know what it is, I'm ready to tackle it head on."

Wanda was right. My imagination had gotten the best of me while we waited for the test results. But now, I was ready to learn everything I needed to know, for my dad and for the rest of us. There was one thing that was still on my mind so I decided to run it by T-Bone and Wanda.

"Listen, guys," I began, "I appreciate everything you're doing to make this easier for my family, and I don't wanna sound ungrateful, but I thought about it and I think I have to retire."

"Nick, I think you have to have a real job before they let you retire," said T-Bone.

"Nick, what are you talking about?" asked Wanda. "Retire from what?"

"From being an *Unofficial Junior Ambassador*," I said. "You guys should do it without me. I'm too distracted with my dad. All I can think about is health stuff."

"You can't retire," said T-Bone. "I'm too young to hang out with a retired guy. Plus, you don't golf. What are you gonna do? Spend all day tinkering in the garage? Or doing crossword puzzles? Or sitting on a bench at the mall with George?"

I almost laughed when he mentioned George. He was such a good friend, and when we met him, it was on a bench at the mall. George had been depressed from losing his wife, and back then, he was really grumpy. After hanging out with us though, he started living his life again. He even hired us for odd-jobs. Besides my grandparents, he was my favorite senior citizen. I imagined how hard George would laugh if I told him I thought about retiring. It sounded good in my head, but saying it out loud, it did sound kind of silly.

"Actually," said Wanda. "I thought you might say that, so I have a solution."

"Now, you can solve problems you think may happen before they even happen?" I asked in amazement.

"Well, yes," she answered. "Anyway, why don't we explore healthy places in New Jersey? It would be the ultimate in multi-tasking!"

It was the most amazing suggestion I had ever heard. The truth was, I never wanted to retire from being an ambassador. I was just afraid I would inadvertently slow them down. Now, I'd be able to help my dad and other kids stay healthy while still sharing New Jersey. It was perfect. Anyway, I really was too young to retire; *especially since I didn't golf.*

Chapter Five

This Is My Pantry, Not a Wawa

Over the next couple of days, we were busy getting healthy. I suddenly realized how much time was involved in being healthy. It wasn't just picking an apple over a candy apple. It was learning how to read a label and actually understand what that information meant. It meant making and eating real food instead of what Pop called "convenient food". Then, there was finding time to be active. I wasn't sure how adults did it with jobs, kids, and taking care of homes. We were kids, with much less responsibility compared to most adults, *and we were having a hard time.* Since my dad's first doctor visit, T-Bone and I realized how inactive we had become once we became ambassadors. In addition to nutrition and exercise, being healthy required things like sleep and lowering stress. It almost sounded like a full-time job. I wondered how busy people ever found time to be healthy. Hopefully, Wanda had the answer.

A few days before we had removed a bunch of unhealthy foods from our pantry. Today, my dad and I were going back in. This time, we were finding the rest of the unhealthy items. While we worked in the pantry, my mom was sitting at the kitchen table creating lists and charts on her laptop. Whenever something was happening, my mom poured herself into lists and charts. It seemed to calm her down.

"Honey, which cereals are we getting rid of?" my dad asked as he held up four brightly-colored, cartoon-character-covered boxes.

"All of them," she said with a smile.

"Seriously?" he asked. "Shouldn't we keep one, just in case of an emergency?"

"A sugary cereal emergency?" she asked without looking up. "Hmmm, I'm gonna go with a no."

"Okay, well which chips should we keep?" He re-emerged holding up several bags of snacks. "The puffy ones are filled with air and because air is just, well, air, they're probably much healthier."

"Seriously?" my mom asked in her most sarcastic tone. "That sounds like a Maggie argument."

"Well, it was worth a try," he shrugged.

While we cleaned out the pantry, then the refrigerator, and then the freezer, my mom made meal plans, shopping lists, and snack suggestions. My dad looked pitiful. He seemed so sad to get rid of some of his favorite snacks and foods. Luckily, the food wasn't going far. Refusing to waste any of it, my mom sent it home with T-Bone.

"What's that?" asked my dad as he looked at my mom's computer screen.

"It's our illustrated snack suggestions," she said with a proud smile.

"Why do we need a list of suggestions with pictures?" he asked. "I think we all know what's healthy and what foods look like. Whenever we picked unhealthy things, it's just because they were there. Now, they're gone."

"Think you know what's healthy?" she said.

"I don't think it's that hard," he said. "You know, they do have labels."

My mom and I stopped and looked at each other. This sounded like a great challenge.

"What's up, healthy people?" asked T-Bone as he entered the kitchen with Wanda behind him.

"I didn't think we were meeting today," I said, wondering why they were standing in my kitchen.

"We know," said T-Bone. "But we wanted to tell you about a few good places that Wanda found..."

"Thanks to some helpful NJ kids," she interrupted.

"And, we also knew you were creating a healthy kitchen," said T-Bone, "so we're here to help."

Wanda sat next to my mom and was impressed with how much she had learned so quickly. And, of course, because she was Wanda, she especially loved the charts. She quickly commented on how great the illustrated snack suggestions were.

"I'm glad you like it," my mom said with a smile. "Mr. A. thinks it's unnecessary because it's easy to pick out healthy snacks if you just read the labels."

"Oh, Mr. A., Mr. A., Mr. A.," Wanda said as she shook her head.

"That's three Mr. A.'s, Mr. A.," whispered T-Bone. "I think that means you're in trouble. Big trouble."

"Mr. A.," said Wanda, sounding just like a teacher, "I'm sure I don't have to tell you that when people look for a snack, they're already hungry and, that hunger can lead to bad choices."

"No, of course you don't have to tell me that," said my dad, making the *"Save-me!"* face.

"And," she continued, "I'm sure I don't have to tell you that food labels are seriously flawed because they use metric, a form of measurement that we don't even understand, right?"

"Of course not," he continued, nodding faster.

"Oh, and I almost forgot," she went on. "I'm sure you know that some food manufacturers use different names for their unhealthy ingredients."

"Absolutely," my dad nodded and then shrugged at the rest of us. "Multiple names, lots of names."

"So that's exactly why this illustrated chart is so

important," she said matter-of-factly. "And the pictures make the visual part of your brain want to eat the healthy food. It's actually very simple."

"Yeah, it's elementary," he laughed.

"What's on the snack list?" asked T-Bone.

My mom held up the list and surprisingly, it looked nice. She'd made healthy foods look even more appealing. There were lots of things, including a bowl of air-popped popcorn, a banana, an apple sliced in wedges and dipped in peanut butter, a bowl of grapes, vegetables and dip, and a bowl of strawberries with whipped cream. At first, I had agreed with my dad. I thought it was useless. Now, seeing how colorful the pictures were, I could see how this would help someone make good choices by giving them good ideas.

"Hey, pretty pictures," said Maggie as she walked into the kitchen. "But, where are the lollipops and ice cream sundaes?"

"This is a list of healthy snack ideas," my mom explained. "The key word is healthy."

"Ice cream is healthy," Maggie insisted. "It has strawberries and chocolate chips."

"Sure," said my mom, "a little ice cream now and then as a treat is okay, but your snacks should really be fuel for your body."

"But I like my fuel to taste good," said Maggie. "I like it to taste like chocolate chips."

"Look at the pretty pictures," Wanda said as she pointed toward the strawberries and whipped cream. "Don't they look delicious?"

"Yes!" Maggie exclaimed. "And they would be more *delicious-er* with chocolate chips."

"But they're healthier without the chocolate chips," said Wanda.

"But they're much more *delicious-er* with chocolate chips," Maggie countered.

This was the exact moment that Wanda learned an important life lesson. Never debate with a little kid. Ever. It took a few minutes for her to figure out that she should just let it go and walk away. She wasn't only used to being right, she was also used to convincing other people that she was right. When it came to Maggie, that was simply not happening. No matter what Wanda said, Maggie was going to answer with two words and those two words were: chocolate chips. It was somewhat refreshing to see Wanda accept defeat graciously.

When the pantry, refrigerator, and freezer were all cleared out, they looked so much bigger. Now, the real challenge: filling the shelves with healthier foods and then finding the time to make those healthier foods. My mom's first job was hanging her illustrated snack sheet. She ran upstairs, came down with a frame, and found the perfect spot.

"Why is it in a frame?" asked Timmy.

"So it'll look nice and stay nice," she answered.

"It looks so good, I think I'd like to place an order for the strawberries and whipped cream," said T-Bone. "Do I just tell you or is there a computer?"

"This isn't Wawa," I laughed.

"Me, too," said Maggie. "I'll have what he's having. Just add chocolate chips to mine."

"I'll take the large popcorn," said Timmy. "Do you get free refills when you order a large?"

"Hold on, guys," my mom quieted the room. "This is not a Wawa or a movie concession stand. I don't even have any of these foods here yet."

"But you put up the sign," said T-Bone. "It's right there. If you don't have the foods, that's kind of false advertising."

"I know that I put the sign up," she explained. "The first step was to clear out the less healthy foods, which took a couple of days, but now it's done. The next step was to make lists and get organized, which, thanks to the American Diabetes Association, went smoother than I anticipated. The step was to make some signs for information and encouragement. Now, the last steps will be shopping, storing, and preparing."

"Oh, okay. Now I see where you went wrong," said T-Bone. "You shouldn't have advertised until you had actually finished and had all of the products."

"Advertised?" she laughed. "I'm not advertising. This isn't a food truck. It's *my pantry*."

"That's actually a good point," said my dad. "If it was a concession stand, we would be selling everything, wouldn't we?"

With that, Maggie opened her play purse, took out a pretend $1000 bill, and ordered chocolate chips.

"Honey, why don't I take your dozen lists and run to my store to get us started?" asked my dad.

"Oh, no," my mom said, throwing her arms over a pile of lists, "they're not just for the grocery store. Some are for lunches, some are for meals, some are for emergencies."

"Are there any pieces of paper over there that tell me what to buy at the grocery store?" he asked.

"No," she smiled and pointed to the wall. "That list is on the Grocery List Clipboard."

"We have a Grocery List Clipboard now?"

"Yes," she explained. "It has all of the main foods we'll need to buy each week to be healthy and then space for add-ons."

"Wonderful time-saver, Mrs. A," said Wanda.

"Okay," my dad said, careful not to criticize my mom after all she was doing to help him. Even though everyone, except Wanda, thought she was going a little overboard, he realized how much work she had been doing. "I'm just going to grab this handy-dandy list and head over to my store. We may as well start our new lifestyle now."

"That's very important," said Wanda.

"Running to the store?" he asked.

"No," she corrected, "it's a good idea to approach this as a lifestyle change, not a diet or a program. You see, if you say 'diet', it sounds negative and like you're giving something up. And what do people want more than anything?"

"Chocolate chips," said Maggie.

"No, no, people want what they can't have," said Wanda. "But, if it's a lifestyle change, it becomes positive and about the options you can have."

"Good point," said my dad, kind of not paying any attention to her. "Alright, I'll be back in... well, as long as it takes me to get these forty-seven pre-numbered items."

"I'll get my shoes," I said, knowing Colonel Coupon couldn't shop without Lieutenant Locator. Even though I moaned about it, helping my dad wasn't that bad. He carried a pouch of coupons and my job was to locate the correct items; right down to size, flavor, and brand.

"Maybe we should all go," said Wanda.

"You want to go to the grocery store with my dad?" I asked, completely shocked.

"Sure, it would be the best place to check out labels," she replied.

"Well, they definitely have labels there," my dad laughed.

"Great," said Wanda. "I'll bring my tablet and we can use the Fooducate app to scan foods."

"Very high tech," said T-Bone.

"We'll definitely need a notebook, though," she suggested.

And there we were, piled into the van with my dad, way too excited to be headed to the grocery store. Who would have thought food shopping would ever be considered exciting?

As we drove the short distance to his store, Wanda decided we needed a strategy. She said we should go through the store and point to things we would like to buy. She would then scan the bar code and if it received a grade of A or B, it went on the good list. If it didn't she would look for an alternative.

"Why are we doing this?" I asked. "You know everything we pick will be considered unhealthy."

"Well, some foods might surprise you," she said, as we entered the store. "And if something you really like gets a bad grade, it will give you a suggestion for something similar, but healthier."

"Yeah, but I have to help my dad with the coupons," I said.

"Don't worry about it," my dad replied. "It looks like most of the things on your mother's list won't have a coupon. Go ahead with your friends."

So while my dad lingered around the perimeter, spending most of his time in his homeland, *the produce section,* we worked the middle of the store.

"Welcome to Factory Food Land," she said as if she'd morphed into a grocery store tour guide. "On your left, you will find that traditional breakfast staple, cereal. Sounds innocent enough, but looks can be deceiving. Don't let the package fool you."
"Hold on," said T-Bone. "I thought the labels were trying to fool us. Which one is it?"

"Actually, it's both," she stated with authority. "These packages are designed to sell a product.

They use bright colors, attractive pictures, and buzz words like *whole grain* and *fortified*."

"What's wrong with *whole grain* and *fortified*?" I asked. "Whole grain sounds healthy and I don't know what fortified means, but it sounds healthy."

"Whole grain isn't bad," she said. "It's a good source of fiber and better than processed grains. But the cereals geared towards kids have other things besides whole grains."

"Oh, you mean a prize in the box?" asked T-Bone, very excited. "I love finding the prize in the box."

"No, T-Bone," she said, shaking her head, "they contain lots of other things."

"Oh, like marshmallows," he interrupted. "I love the marshmallows. Once my mom bought a box of cereal that was all marshmallows. I don't know why she never bought it again."

"T-Bone, the marshmallows are mostly sugar," said Wanda. "And they're also full of artificial colors and preservatives."

"But the colors make it look good and turn the milk cool colors," he insisted.

"So are you saying we should stay away from cereals with colors and marshmallows?" I asked, a little disappointed.

"Let's read the labels and then you can decide for yourselves," she suggested.

As we scanned box after box, I noticed a pattern. The cereals with the kid-friendly packages and characters, the cereals with the catchy songs and commercials, and the cereals with the prizes and games on the box...*they weren't honor roll cereals.* They were mostly C's and D's. Some had two and a half teaspoons of sugar in each serving and a serving was only ¾ of a cup. Wanda had actually brought a set of measuring cups and spoons in her drawstring bag. When she held up the ¾ cup, we were shocked. T-Bone said it would take at least three of them to fill up his favorite cereal bowl. I hated to admit it, but I often ate two bowls of cereal and each was more than that little serving.

"This is depressing," I said. "When kids see the commercials and the bright boxes, they want the cereals and when parents see those buzz words, they think they can't be that bad."

"Exactly," said Wanda.

"You know when I was a kid, we ate things like eggs for breakfast," said a familiar voice.

We turned around and saw our friend, George, standing there with his shopping cart. I didn't know how long he had been standing there, but he seemed amused.

"Hey George," we all said at the same time.

"Well, well, well," he laughed. "What do we have here? A cereal convention?"

We filled him in on our newest cause and told him about my dad. He nodded patiently as he listened and told us that he knows many people with Type 2 diabetes. He said he couldn't be prouder of us.

"Why are you so proud?" asked T-Bone. "We're not doing anything amazing. We're just following Wanda and her scanner around the store."

"No, Tommy," he said, "the fact that you are paying attention to nutrition and not only helping your dad, but bringing this information to your school is wonderful. You can help a lot of people."

"I don't know," I said. "It will be easier to give my dad boring cereal because he has to eat it. I think it will be way harder to tell kids to give up the fun, bright-colored, marshmallow cereals."

"Might not be as hard as you think," he said as he shook his head. "Let me ask you a question. As you're learning about what's really in your food, is it making you think twice about eating it?"

"Kinda," I said. "But the healthier cereals are probably boring."

"I'll tell you a little secret," said George. "Sugar is addictive. And once you get used to eating so many foods high in sugar, these other healthier foods don't taste as good."

"Then we're doomed?" asked T-Bone. "I mean everyone eats sugar."

"No," George laughed. "If you eat a lot of sugar, your body craves sugar. When you eat things with less sugar, they don't taste as good. But if you lower the sugar you eat, the cravings go away and things with less sugar taste better."

"So we have to eat the cereals in boring boxes?" asked T-Bone.

"Honestly, some of these healthy cereals taste

great," he continued. "You should look for whole grain, fiber, and low sugar. Some of these other cereals have as much sugar as a candy bar."

"So should we just eat a candy bar for breakfast, instead?" asked T-Bone.

"No, T-Bone," Wanda scolded. "What he's trying to tell you is that some of these cereals are as healthy as a candy bar. There are so many cereals here and breakfast is the most important meal of the day. We should try to pick good ones."

"And," George added, "there's plenty of things to eat in the morning besides cereal."

"True," I agreed. "Didn't you say you ate eggs every morning? Is that healthier?"

"Well, eggs have protein, which fills you up better and keeps you full longer," he explained. "You see, back when I was a boy, most moms stayed at home and they had time to cook us hot breakfasts like eggs, oatmeal, pancakes, and things like that. Now, it often takes two parents working just to survive, so there isn't time to make a big meal before school and work."

"Yeah," I laughed, "my mom brings so much work

home that she barely cooks dinner some days."

"Exactly," said George. "That's why you have to be smart with your choices. You can have a yogurt with fresh fruit, wheat toast, a little jam, eggs..."

"Ooh, you can also have muffins or donuts," said T-Bone. "They're fast and delicious."

"But are they nutritious?" asked George.

"Let's see," said Wanda as she headed right over to the packaged baked goods aisle. "Here we go."

The chocolate chip muffins she scanned got a C on the Fooducate site. They were highly processed, had no whole grains, and had 4.5 teaspoons of sugar. Next, a box of donuts with 4 teaspoons of sugar, no whole grains, highly processed, and 20% of daily saturated fat. I wasn't sure what that meant, but it sounded like a lot for a small donut.

"Besides your app, there is something else you should look at," said George.

"The price?" I asked.

"No," he smiled. "The ingredients."

We turned the boxes over and couldn't believe it. The lists of ingredients on both boxes were huge. For small items, there were so many of them.

"You know what all of those ingredients means?" asked T-Bone. "These must be a good value. How can they buy all of those ingredients and still sell this box for under $5.00? We should get two."

George laughed. He told us that his wife, Martha, made homemade muffins for his family and the ingredients were flour, sugar, egg, salt, baking soda, butter, milk and chocolate chips. When T-Bone pointed out that they had sugar, George reminded him that while they did have sugar, they didn't have chemicals, preservatives, or artificial colors, and his wife made small muffins. The portion size was smaller and they didn't eat them every day. They were a treat, not a daily snack.

"Oh, so your kids ate three or four?" asked T-Bone.

"No," George shook his head. "Portion sizes were much smaller. We were used to healthy portions. What restaurants serve now is quite often the equivalent of three meals worth of food. Then they often load the foods with extra fat and sugar to keep people coming back for more."

While we headed to the cracker and chip aisle, George said good-bye and asked us to stop over and help him with some errands when we had time. He also offered to volunteer at our health fair, although he did have one suggestion. He told us we needed a new name for it. He said a health fair sounded as exciting as getting his teeth cleaned. He said we should grab kids' attention and offered a great suggestion: a Fitness Fun Fair.

When we finally caught up to my dad, he told us he really didn't get much from the middle of the store. He had lots of fresh and whole foods and he seemed excited. Of course, Wanda checked out the cart, probably at my mom's request. Luckily, she approved of everything.

The whole ride home we told my dad about what we learned. Rather than just saying "uh-huh" like he often did, he was very interested in what we were telling him. Wanda even had an idea for him. She told him he should place healthy recipe cards near the vegetables and show attractive, bright pictures of the fruits to get people more interested.

"Like an illustrated snack sheet?" he laughed.

"Exactly," she nodded. *"Just like an illustrated snack sheet!"*

Chapter Six

Great Ideas Keep Coming

I hated to admit it, but our trip to the grocery store was actually fun. And what an eye-opener. I knew it would take a while for us to completely understand and implement everything, but I definitely felt like we were on the right track. And even better, my mom and dad seemed more excited to make these changes than overwhelmed.

The next day, we decided to follow up on Wanda's idea to combine New Jersey and fitness. We knew, from our Garden State Adventures, that New Jersey had an amazing Great Outdoors and so many of our trips were places where you could be active. Now, we just needed to go through the new suggestions from Billy to find some good matches.

Billy was our contact at the State House and he was the reason we had become Unofficial Junior Ambassadors. Well, it wasn't Billy's idea, but as soon as he was assigned to help us, he constantly steered us in the right direction. From finding Allyssa Barnes, creator of the www.nickyfifth.com website, to sending us fan mail and suggestions from kids, to surprising us by showing up at T-Bone's debate to become class president. The one thing that he couldn't help us with, though, was the bills to name us *Official Junior Ambassadors*. While I wanted it to happen really badly, T-Bone was devastated that they'd never gotten around to voting for us. We worked so hard to share New Jersey with New Jersey families and often wondered why they didn't see the good we were doing. T-Bone was crushed when it didn't happen and, even though he didn't talk about it as much anymore, I knew it still bothered him and tried not to bring it up.

In the meantime, we had work to do. When Wanda arrived, she had a folder filled with submissions. We looked through the pile and were amazed by how many great ideas kept coming. For a small state, we were overflowing with quality locations.

"So, guys, this is gonna be tough," said Wanda.

"It always is," I laughed. "What have we got?"

"Well, a girl named Ella Deuber from Bass River Elementary in Tuckerton wrote about the New Gretna Mansion which sounds like a mysterious property with a wall surrounding it," said T-Bone as he skimmed her submission. "There are many amazing and interesting statues all around it. They even have statues of a giraffe and two elephants. She said it was a great place."

"Sounds like my kind of mansion," I said. "Instead of stuffy, it sounds fun."

"We have two kids who wrote about a place called Butterhof's Farm in Egg Harbor City," Wanda read. "Carlene Mains and Francesco Randazzo, from Mullica Township School, wrote about the corn maze, pumpkin patch, and field trips. They said it was a great place to have pictures taken, so it must be really pretty."

"Hey, here's a good one," I said as I grabbed the next one off the top of the pile, "it's about one of my favorite places. Zoey Askins, also from Mullica Township School, wrote about amazing, historic Batsto Village and Museum."

"That is an awesome place," said T-Bone. "And

historic, too! Our trips there have been great."

"Here's one from one of our very favorite places, Wildwood," I said as I read the next submission. "It's from Emily Evans at McKinley Avenue School in Stafford Township and it perfectly describes the excitement of Wildwood."

"Did she mention the water parks?" asked T-Bone.

"Yup," I nodded.

"The rides and the boardwalk?" he asked.

"Of course," I said, remembering how much fun we had when my mom brought us there for a real adventure. The best part was that we were so exhausted, but my mom kept on going.

"Hey, guys, this is interesting," said Wanda. "I've never heard of this place. It's called the Info Age Museum and it's dedicated to the history of communication. It sounds incredible. It's from Lucas Zapatas-Sanin from Stony Brook School in Hopewell Township."

"That definitely has to go on our list of places to visit!" I said and we all agreed. "I also love the address, it's on Marconi Road in Wall Township."

"Do you mean Macaroni Road?" asked T-Bone.

"No, it's Marconi," I laughed. "Don't you remember Marconi invented the wireless radio?"

"That's a great stroke of luck that the museum is on a street named after him," T-Bone exclaimed.

"I don't think it was a coincidence," Wanda sighed as she rolled her eyes and grabbed the next submission. "This one is also from Stony Brook and it's from Ishan Gupta. Ishan wrote about the Governor's mansion."

"Which one?" I asked. "Drumthwacket or Morven?"

"Neither," she laughed.

"I don't get it," I said. "It has to be one of them."

"Actually," said Wanda, "it's about The Proprietary House, the house for the last Royal Governor."

"Wow, that must be old," said T-Bone.

"Hey, we learned about the last Royal Governor when we were in Burlington," I said as I tried to remember. Then it came to me. "Wasn't Ben Franklin's son, William Franklin, the last Royal

Governor of New Jersey, and didn't he side with the King of England as a loyalist?"

"Oh, yeah, that's right," T-Bone remembered. "He picked the wrong side and ended up with a one-way ticket back to England."

"He signed the charter for Queens College," I read.

"I wouldn't have thought there was enough royalty in the world to have a college just for them," T-Bone pondered.

"No, it wasn't a college for Kings and Queens," I laughed. "And it eventually became Rutgers University, the state university. Remember, when we took our tour through New Brunswick with Alexi Garcia?"

"Yeah, that's right," said T-Bone. "Remember we met that storm chaser Joe at the Grease Trucks?"

"Oh yeah," I nodded. "We really have covered a lot of the state, haven't we?"

"That's why making every kid in New Jersey an ambassador with us was so brilliant," said T-Bone. "They're making us smarter!"

"This is one I love," said Wanda. "It's the Princeton University Art Museum. And, this is also from a student at Stony Brook. The student is Abhijay Singireddy. I have to agree with Abhijay, that museum has an amazing collection and it's so relaxing. It's a great place to just sit back and take in the art and the atmosphere."

"How do you know?" asked T-Bone.

"Been there," she smirked. "You know I did go to some New Jersey places before I met you guys. Now, what else do we have?"

"Well, this one isn't relaxing," I said, "although it's also from a Stony Brook student! It's from Leo Huang and he wrote about the South Mountain Recreation Area in West Orange. It sounds great. They have a Treetop Adventure Course for zip lining with 30 challenges, paddle boats, mini-golf, an ice arena and hold on, McLoones. Wait a minute, that's the restaurant where we met with Governor Brendan Byrne."

"How did we miss all of this stuff?" asked T-Bone.

"I don't know," I laughed, "as I recall, you were just a little excited to meet Governor Byrne."

"That's true, T-Bone," said Wanda, "you were beyond excited."

"Come on, Wanda," I laughed, "you were wearing ruffles from head to toe. Admit it, we were all so excited to meet a former governor."

"Not just any former governor," said T-Bone. "The man who saved one million acres in the pinelands with the Pinelands Preservation Act. He protected one of New Jersey's most valuable natural resources. And he ate french fries off my plate. *It was a perfect day!*"

We laughed about how excited and nervous we were and how Gov. Byrne made us so comfortable. I knew that was a day I would never forget.

"Speaking of preservation," said Wanda, "Faith Carhuff from Lloyd Road School in Aberdeen wrote about a place called Bayonet Farm and talked about an exciting location that has an amazing Earth Day celebration. She said it's located in Holmdel and has 240-acres, historic buildings like the 1930 Red Barn, bird sanctuaries, a historic house, a horticulture garden, and a petting zoo."

"You know who'd like that place?" asked T-Bone.

"Who?" Wanda and I said together.

"BTB," T-Bone replied.

"Who's BTB?" I asked.

"Hello!" he said, as though we weren't keeping up. "Gov. Brendan T. Byrne, my personal friend."

"This sounds pretty cool," I said. "Shane Deman, from Mullica Township School, wrote about the Mullica River, canoeing, and kayaking. There was also fishing and the relaxing peace and quiet."

"We should check that out," said Wanda. "Wellness isn't just nutrition, it's also fitness and relaxation. That river seems to have both; unless T-Bone tries to walk on wet rocks like at the Lockwood Gorge!"

"Well, when he fell in, it made us laugh and they say laughter is good for stress reduction," I said.

He mentioned the history of the area, like the Battle of Chestnut Neck when the British Army bombarded the Patriots at the mouth of the river. Then he told us about a guy named Joe Mulliner who was known as the Robin Hood of Mullica. That sounded like some interesting history.

"Now, this sounds amazing," said Wanda, "and guess who it's from?"

"A student from Stony Brook?" I laughed.

"Actually, the librarian, Marci Thomas, attached a note," said Wanda. "She said her students follow all of our adventures and she even created Google Earth Tours of the places we go."

"No wonder they're all sending us ideas," I noted.

"No, way," said T-Bone. "How did she know when we would be at those places?"

"The tours aren't pictures of us visiting those places," I laughed. "They're just pictures of the places we visit, but in a digital tour."

"That's cool," said T-Bone. "Even if we're not in it."

"Well, anyway," said Wanda, "Sarah Miller Piotrowski wrote about a place called The Brothers Moon. It's a farm-to-table restaurant that makes healthy food taste fabulous."

"That's a perfect place to check out," I agreed. "Maybe my mom can get some ideas."

"It gets better," she continued. "They change the menu every few weeks to keep things fresh and different, the service is over the top, and there's a historic house with an outside sitting area."

"Let's go tonight," said T-Bone. "How about we call your grandfather?"

"No," I shook my head, "let's wait and try to get my mom or both of my parents to go on that one."

"Good point," said T-Bone.

"Hey," I said, "two kids from McKinley School in Stafford Township, Matthew Desiderio and Nolan Friend, wrote about Tuckerton."

"We loved Tuckerton," said T-Bone.

"They say to check out the Truckerton Festival."

"You mean Tuckerton Food Festival," said T-Bone.

"It's actually the Truck-erton Food Truck Festival," I laughed. "It sounds awesome. This also reminds me of the Grease Trucks at Rutgers University."

"Add it to the list," said T-Bone, rubbing his stomach. "I'm suddenly in the mood for truck food."

"Adding," I confirmed.

"Wow, this next place must be very cool," said T-Bone as he held up three papers. "Three kids from Stony Brook wrote about the Duke Farms in Hillsborough. Fiona Fan, Alex Boccumini, and Briana Mahilo wrote about its history, the nature, the relaxation, and the activities of the farm."

"Sounds like a homerun," I said. "And, it also has something for everyone."

"They have 2,700 acres and you can hike, bike, and run. If you don't have a bike, you can rent one," T-Bone continued. "They say there's plenty of space to relax and think and, Nick, your dad will like this, it's free."

"Another grand slam," I laughed. "Let's get some more details and see if we can go."

"Hold on, I have a really great piece here by Eden Collins from Normandy Park School located in Morristown," said Wanda. "She suggests we visit Fosterfields Living History Farm."

"I wonder if it's like that farm we visited in Hopewell, the Howell Living History Farm," I said.

"Probably," she smiled. "It sounds amazing. It's a 19th century working farm with exhibits, volunteers wearing period clothing, and hands-on activities. I think we should check this out."

"Sounds good to me," said T-Bone. "Especially since this is the Garden State and we literally have thousands of farms. Seeing how farming used to be is a great way to add history to agriculture. Where's it located?"

"It's in Morristown," replied Wanda.

"Wait a minute," I said. "I have an idea for a long, fun-filled day."

"Go ahead," said Wanda, eager to hear my idea.

"Okay, we leave very early and go straight to the Fosterfields Farm. Next, we head south. It should only take about forty minutes or so to get to Duke Farms and then, hold on. It's only about a half hour to The Brothers Moon."

"That's brilliant," said Wanda.

"It's smart," said T-Bone, suddenly sounding a little jealous, "but I wouldn't say brilliant."

"Well, I would," Wanda replied with a little sneer. "I'll take care of the planning, unless you want to."

"Nope, we're good," T-Bone and I said together.

Bringing Wanda on board had really spoiled us.

"You know, I was thinking," said Wanda. "George was right. We really should call it the *Fitness Fun Fair* to excite everyone."

"I agree," I nodded.

"Totally agree," said T-Bone.

"But I think we need to focus on all aspects of wellness," she continued. "Nutrition's huge, but sleep, activity and stress management are also huge."

"Do kids need stress management?" asked T-Bone.

"Everyone does," said Wanda. "Stress is a part of life and schools have never been more stressful."

"My dad always says to enjoy the stress-free days of childhood before we have the responsibilities of being an adult," replied T-Bone. "I'm starting to think it's too late."

"Well, it's true, adults do have a lot of stress," Wanda explained. "But kids have a lot of stress, too. There's schoolwork, friends, family issues, and sometimes medical issues. I think if you learn to be well as a kid, it will carry through when you're an adult and life gets even more stressful."

"That's a good point," I said, T-Bone glaring at me. "Maybe we should come up with a way for kids to track their efforts," suggested Wanda. "I asked my mom to buy me a step counter so I can keep track of how many steps I walk."

"How do you know if you walked enough?" I asked.

"They say we should walk 10,000 steps in a day," she answered. "They also say kids should have one hour of activity each day."

"One hour of exercise?" asked T-Bone. "That's not just push-ups, is it?"

"Actually, I don't think we should call it exercise," said Wanda. "Exercise sounds like a chore. After money, it's the thing adults complain about most."

"True," T-Bone agreed. "My mom hates to exercise. She feels better when she's done, but it's definitely not her favorite thing to do."

"Exactly," said Wanda. "We have to make sure kids know that activity isn't just walking on a treadmill or doing jumping jacks. It can be fun."

"My grandfather is always telling me about the games he played with his friends when he was a kid," I added. "He used to teach them to me and my friends in Philly. It never seemed like exercise, but we sure sweated when we played."

"That's what I'm talking about," she said. "Can you make a list of games? You too, T-Bone. And I'll try to design a chart that kids can use to keep track of things like how many hours they slept, how much activity they completed, and things like that."

"Um, Pop didn't teach me any games," said T-Bone. "But I can find more healthy places to visit."

"Sounds good to me," said Wanda.

"Me, too," I agreed.

As we packed up, T-Bone's mood improved quickly and I knew exactly why. It was his favorite time of day. The time when he walked Wanda home. If Wanda got a step tracker it would be even more exciting for him...*then he would know exactly how many steps they shared.*

Chapter Seven

Fruits and Vegetables? A Luxury?

Later that night, I told my parents about all of the submissions and our ideas to incorporate activity, sleep, and stress management. My mom totally agreed with replacing the word "exercise". She said that except for the rare people who loved to work out, most people dreaded it, which was probably why most people avoided it. She loved the idea of using Pop's games and said that anytime you make something fun- whether it's schoolwork, eating healthy, or even exercise- people get more out of it. And, they'll also continue with it, which, she told us, was really the most important thing.

My dad seemed to really like the idea of a step counter. He even went online to see how much they cost and he was pleasantly surprised that they weren't very expensive. Obviously, you could spend a ton of money on them, but you didn't have to. If you simply wanted to know how many steps you walked, calories you burned, distance, and time, you could get them pretty cheap.

"You know what?" he said, "I'm buying everyone a pedometer."

"What's that?" I asked.

"A step counter," my mom laughed. "But, hon, who's everyone?"

"Well," he said slowly, "me, you, Nicky, Timmy, and I guess T-Bone and Wanda."

"Really?" I asked. While our bodies use insulin to unlock our cells, my dad's diabetes seemed to have unlocked his wallet.

"Really," my dad nodded.

"You forgot one," I added.

"Maggie and Emma are too young," said my dad, somewhat confused.

"No, not them," I said. "I meant Pop. He comes on so many of our trips, let's include him."

"Okay," my dad said, "I'll order seven of them."

"If Wanda is making a tracking sheet, let's do it as a group," my mom suggested. "Let's track our steps and cheer each other on."

"That's a great idea," I said.

"They say it works better when you have a buddy," she laughed. "Imagine what can happen when we each have six buddies."

"Sky's the limit," my dad laughed and shook his head. "Listen, I really appreciate what you're all doing. The whole positive spin and working to be healthy as a group is good stuff. Really good stuff."

"Wait until the whole school's on board," I laughed.

"Except, I'm not buying hundreds of pedometers," he exclaimed as he held up his hand.

There's the dad I knew, I laughed to myself.

"You know, Nicky," said my mom. "There are some other wellness areas you should explore."

"Like what?" I asked.

"I saw a report about sunscreen," she said. "I don't think people realize how important it is to not only apply it whenever you're going outside, but to keep reapplying it. Many people never apply it or only apply once. The sun can really damage your skin."

"Then, why in all of the pictures of you and Dad as kids, are you both as red as lobsters?" I laughed.

"Believe it or not," she said with a smile, "back then, people thought a bad sunburn *was healthy*."

"Ouch," I said. "That sounds like an awful idea."

"Not only that," she continued. "We would lay out in the sun for hours trying to get more sun."

"Sounds hot and boring," I laughed.

"Oh, it was," she nodded. "But now that we know how harmful the sun's rays can be, you should include that message. If kids start protecting their skin when they're young, they can avoid serious issues when they're older."

"Good idea," I agreed. "Ben Franklin was right."

"Don't fly a kite in a storm?" she asked.

"No, an ounce of prevention's worth a pound of cure."

"Words to live by," she smiled. "Words to live by."

"I didn't know you could buy prevention and cures by the ounce and the pound," said Timmy. "Does everybody know about this?"

"Timmy," my mom sighed, "it's a saying that means it costs less money and takes less time to be careful and prevent a problem, than it does to fix a problem after it has happened."

"Oh," he said. "The kite and storm one is better."

As excited as I was about our upcoming adventures, I still wanted to learn more about diabetes. I started randomly Googling words related to diabetes. The information was shocking. The number of people living with diabetes, world-wide, is increasing. The International Diabetes Federation predicted the number to rise from 366 million people in 2011 to 552 million people by 2030. In the United States alone, the number had doubled over the last thirty years. If that wasn't scary enough, the website said it was mostly due to obesity. Since the 1960s, obesity in the United

States, for kids and adults, had doubled. I wondered why and thought about what George had said. He told us that people had more time to prepare healthy meals when he was a kid.

I kept reading and found my answer. The obesity epidemic was complicated. There wasn't one cause; there were multiple causes. There was the amount of food and drinks people were consuming, the amount of meals eaten outside of the home, portion sizes increased, and less time for activity. It made sense and because obesity was the cause of things like diabetes and heart disease, they were rising also. Even things like Celiac Disease, a reaction of the immune system to eating gluten, a protein found in wheat, barley, and rye, was now four times more common than it was fifty years ago.

"How's the research coming?" asked my mom.

"It's crazy," I said. "In some places, people get sick and die because they don't have enough food."

"I know," she nodded. "It's heartbreaking. We forget how lucky we are to have what we have."

"Mom," I began, "in our country, people are getting diseases and dying because we have too much food and we don't make smart choices."

When I told her about everything I'd found, she plopped down on the couch. "You know, Nicky, you're right. The only difference is; we should know better. Imagine how much healthier and happier everyone would be if we learned to ignore the commercials and fancy packages and selected good foods in the right amounts. Imagine how much heartbreak could be avoided from watching people you love suffer. And then think about all of the money our whole country would save if we weren't treating all of these avoidable diseases."

"You know what's scary, Mom?" I continued. "In almost every case of Type 2 diabetes, the person had prediabetes first."

"Wow," she said, shaking her head, "we might have been able to help your father sooner."

"But it says there are no clear symptoms, so you may not even know you have it," I read.

"We have several kids in my school with Type 1 diabetes," she noted. "Our school nurse discussed it with the staff at the beginning of the year. It used to be called Juvenile Diabetes and only 5% of diabetes patients have this form of the disease."

"What's the difference?" I asked.

"Well, if I remember correctly," she explained, "in Type 1, the body doesn't make any insulin."

"No key to open cells and let glucose in?" I asked.

"No, honey," she replied, "no key. That's why they frequently test their blood sugar levels and part of their treatment is insulin therapy."

"With all of our technology and advances, why are some diseases getting so much worse?" I wondered.

"Well, all of our technology isn't very helpful when it comes to being active," she explained. "Previous generations had to do so much more, physically, than we have to do. When I was a kid, we didn't even have a remote control so we had to get up to constantly change the channel."

"That must have taken forever," I gasped.

"Not really," she laughed. "Before cable, we only had about a dozen channels."

"That must have been so boring," I said.

"Actually, it was," she agreed, "but that made us more creative. And, more physical. When there was nothing good on TV, we went outside and played. Remember, we didn't have the internet or video games. We ran around and played together."

"Pop's games?" I asked.

"Pop's games," she nodded.

"What else was different?" I asked.

"We didn't have a dishwasher, so we stood by the sink after dinner. Someone washed, someone dried and we talked the whole time," she said.

"I guess those little things really added up," I said.

"I guess they did," she sighed. "You know what else has increased? Autism. So many more children are on the Autism Spectrum now. In 2000, it was 1 out of every 150 kids, now it's 1 out of every 68 kids."

"Why?" I asked.

"They don't know what causes it, and the spike in numbers could just be better diagnosing," she said. "And a wider definition that now includes more kids. Other than that, I'm not sure."

"Hopefully, our Fitness Fun Fair will make kids more aware," I said.

"Is the whole school on board?" she asked.

"Ms. Swanson said the school nurse and gym teachers wanna be involved in planning the event," I said. "And the custodians, secretaries, cafeteria workers, and bus drivers are in, too."

"Well, I think anything you do to raise awareness and motivate people to make changes is worth it."

While my mom went upstairs, I went back to my research. Just as I was about to take a break, I stumbled upon something unbelievable. It was a show called *Austin the Unstoppable* and it was about a boy named Austin whose mom is diagnosed with Type 2 diabetes. Except for the mom and dad difference, Austin's story was almost identical to mine. The show could come to your school or you could go to the George Street Playhouse in New Brunswick to see it. I remembered that theater from our New Brunswick tour with Alexi Garcia. I kept reading. I was so excited, I called Wanda and T-Bone to tell them I had found something amazing. Before I hung up with Wanda, T-Bone was standing behind me.

"What's up?" he asked. "Sorry it took me so long, I couldn't find my shoes."

"That was long?" I asked. "We just hung up."

"Hey, guys," said Wanda as she placed her tote bag on the couch. "What have we got?"

"This is amazing," I began. "It's a show called *Austin the Unstoppable* and it's a musical about learning how to make healthy lifestyle choices. They have actually put the message we want to share, to music. Seriously, it's a show about making healthy choices, designed for kids!"

"Really?" asked Wanda. "Tell me more."

"Okay there's a kid named Austin," I continued, "and it says here that he is the master of the X-box and a junk food junkie. He must face the long-term consequences of an unhealthy lifestyle when his mom is diagnosed with Type 2 Diabetes."

"Nick, Nick!" T-Bone exclaimed. "Do you realize if you switch the mother with the father and subtract the video games, that could be your life?"

"Of course, I do," I laughed. "And not only do they have the show, they have resources for kids and teachers, a cool website, and tons of information."

"How did you find it?" asked Wanda, pulling up the

website. "This is outstanding! I wish we could see the show. Where's it located?"

"That's the best part," I said. "They're in New Jersey."

"No way!" T-Bone exclaimed as he pushed me off the chair. "Oops, sorry, Nick."

"You can see the show at the Playhouse or you can have them come to your school," I announced.

"Hold on," said T-Bone. "George Street Playhouse, George Street Playhouse, why does that sound familiar?"

"Alexi Garcia," I said with a smile.

"That's it!" he gasped. "Wanda, this was before you started working with us. Alexi Garcia is our friend from New Brunswick and he gave us an amazing tour for our report. He showed us the playhouse."

"Nicky, this is incredible," Wanda said without taking her eyes off of the tablet. "There's a Dr. Klein who gives great tips like eating a variety of fresh foods, mostly vegetables. He says we should eat three servings of vegetables and two servings of fruits every day."

"Well, we know where we find those foods," I laughed.

"In the refrigerator?" asked T-Bone.

"No, I meant along the perimeter of the grocery store," I replied. "Along the walls, in produce."

"Actually," said Wanda, "there are a couple of other places in the store to find produce."

"On the loading dock?" I asked.

"No," she shook her head. "In the canned food aisle and also in the frozen food section."

"But isn't fresh produce better?" I wondered.

"Believe it or not," my mom said as she walked by, "it has less to do with how you get your vegetables and more to do with what you do with them."

"What do you mean?"

"Well, take corn," she began, "whether it's fresh, frozen, or canned, if you steam it, it will be healthy. But if you cover it in butter and salt, it's not as healthy."

"Kind of like salad?" I asked.

"Exactly," she smiled. "Take a plain, medium-size baked potato. A potato is a whole food, and filled with nutrients. If you bake it, it's healthy. If you bake it and top it with cheddar cheese, bacon, and sour cream, then it's not so healthy."

"Mom, wouldn't Dad be upset if you told people to buy frozen or canned vegetables?" I asked. "Since, you know, he is the produce manager of his store."

"Not at all, honey," she smiled. "He wants everyone to eat fresh vegetables, but it's not always very convenient. Frozen and canned vegetables last longer and they're often more economical. They're especially important to families on a tight budget."

"That's a good point," said Wanda, "nutrition is such a challenge for families that live in poverty. When we were at the grocery store, it seemed like the healthier foods were much more expensive and the fresh foods don't last too long."

"Exactly," my mom nodded. "That's really a huge challenge for families that are struggling. Fresh fruits and vegetables are a luxury that many families cannot afford."

"That's so unfair," I said.

"Plus," my mom continued, "many impoverished families don't have transportation to get to large grocery stores so they shop at small corner stores."

"That sounds nice," said T-Bone. "Very charming."

"Nice and expensive," my mom explained. "Those small stores are great for picking up a few things, but the choices are limited and the prices are very expensive."

"That's terrible," said Wanda. "If they can't stretch the little money they have, they can't be healthy."

"I did read about some cities bringing in farmer's markets to provide residents with an opportunity to buy some fresh produce," said my mom. "And some cities even have community gardens."

As soon as my mom told us about urban farmer's markets and community gardens, I turned and looked at Wanda. Without even speaking, she knew what I was about to say. It was like she was a mind-reader sometimes.

"I'm on it," she said.

When my mom left, we returned to *Austin the Unstoppable*. Dr. Klein also said that we should eat slowly, chew thoroughly, and listen for the *"I'm full"* signal. He suggested drinking more water and finding a way to be active every day. We decided we would start printing everything from the website and share it with Ms. Swanson. My mom asked us to print a copy of everything so she could share it with her principal. She was hoping to invite the show to her school.

As overwhelming as all of this was becoming, there was one particular sentence on the website, from Dr. Klein, that convinced me how important this was. It said that we were the first generation of kids in the United States to live shorter and less healthy lives than our parents. I had already heard a man on the news say our generation would have less money and less opportunities than previous generations. Now this?

Not on my watch, I thought. Not on my watch.

Chapter Eight

It's a Whistle

We were so excited about finding *Austin the Unstoppable* that we decided to use that energy and work on the games together. Before we started, T-Bone ran home. He said he would be back in a minute and I figured he was just dousing himself in his dad's aftershave. When he returned, I didn't smell him walk in. Strange, I thought. Before I could ask what he ran home for, I had my answer. A loud whistle nearly made me fall off my chair, again.

"What is that?" I asked.

"It's a whistle," he said as if I had just arrived from a faraway planet.

"I know what it is," I said.

"Then why'd you ask?" he smirked.

"Okay, I guess I should have said why are you wearing a whistle?" I replied.

"Because I am now officially Coach T-Bone," he announced. "Ready to turn video gamers and couch potatoes into lean, mean wellness machines."

"Really?" asked Wanda. Then in a deep army-like voice she said, "GIVE ME TEN!"

"I'm a little short this week," he answered. "I only have three dollars."

"NOT DOLLARS!" she hollered. "PUSHUPS! DROP AND GIVE ME TEN!"

We both looked shocked. Wanda suddenly turned into a drill sergeant. T-Bone didn't know what to do so he dropped and worked on giving her one. While his grunting sounded impressive, after thirty seconds he was still an inch off the floor.

"I'M WAITING," she hollered.

I couldn't help but laugh. That turned out to be a

big mistake. As soon as I started laughing, she forgot about T-Bone and turned her attention toward me.

"YOU, TOO, FIFTH!" she pointed at me. "DROP AND GIVE ME TEN!"

Luckily, I could manage to do a few, which was better than T-Bone. While I completed my third pushup, T-Bone just grunted louder.

"Enough," she said in her normal voice. "Get up. You proved my point."

"What was your point?" I asked.

"That we all need to be more active," she insisted.

While I stood up, T-Bone rolled onto his back. "Nick, give me a hand," he begged.

He looked like a turtle on his shell. Wow, I thought, we really do need to be more active.

"Okay, Nicky," she said. "Tell us about the fun games that your grandfather taught you when you lived in Philly. Remember your mom said the activities have to be fun if people are going to continue to do them."

"I changed my mind," said T-Bone as he clawed his way up from the floor. "Can't we just have the Senate and Assembly pass an exercise law?"

"A law?" Wanda laughed. "That wouldn't work."

"Why not?" he wondered.

"Well, first of all, I don't know how you enforce an exercise law. Second, the goal is to make people want to exercise. We need to actually motivate, not legislate. And third of all, that's just ridiculous."

"Tell him how you really feel," I laughed.

"Okay, Nick," said T-Bone. "Get us started. Hit us with the Pop games. But don't really hit us."

Wanda took out a notebook as I started talking about the games I played on Fifth Street in Philly with Joey Grapes, Benny Bones, Gino Pie, Bobby Boots, Crazy John, and Freddie Kohler.

"When we were much younger, we used to play games like red light, green light," I started.

"Your parents let you play in an intersection?" T-Bone gasped in horror. "I have to say, I'm a little shocked. That sounds dangerous."

"Of course, it would be dangerous," I exclaimed. "But we didn't play in an actual intersection. One kid was the stop light and the rest of us tried to reach the chalk line where he stood. When he said green, we'd start moving. When he turned around and shouted red light, we had to stop. If we were still moving when he turned around, we were out. If you made it to the chalk line without getting caught, you won."

"Did you win a prize?" he asked.

"No, we didn't win a prize," I snapped. "We played for fun, not for prizes."

"Not even a virtual prize?" he wondered.

"Anyway," I continued, "we also played hide and seek, tag, and *buck-buck-moose*."

"Hold on," Wanda stopped me. "You mean duck-duck-goose, right?"

"No, Benny Bones was afraid of birds and screamed the whole time," I explained. "So his mom asked us to play buck-buck-moose instead. We didn't care. Ducks and geese or deer and moose, it was all the same."

"What else did you play?" she asked.

"Sometimes we would set up obstacle courses and time ourselves," I remembered.

"Like on those ninja warrior shows?" asked T-Bone. "With water pits and climbing walls and using the rings to get to the next level?"

"Yeah, but it wasn't quite so fancy," I laughed. "We used whatever we could, old boxes, hula hoops, sometimes we even had a few tires."

"What else?" he asked.

"We played a lot of kickball in the funeral home parking lot across the street," I remembered. "And wiffle ball, dodge ball, and run the bases."

"Hold on," said T-Bone, "you actually played in a funeral home parking lot? That's kinda creepy."

"Not when there was a funeral," I laughed. "They let us play there if the orange cones weren't out."

"Did you ever see a, you know, a, you know," he said very quietly.

"Do you mean a dead body?" I asked.

"Yeah, I just didn't want to say it," he replied.

"We saw them all the time," I answered. "They brought them in tied to the roof of the hearse."

"Really?" he gasped.

"No, not really," I said, shaking my head. "Of course we didn't see any bodies."

I caught a glimpse of Wanda who was speechless. "How do you play run the bases?" she asked, taking a detour around the dead body topic.

"Well, on the sidewalk, you had two guys standing about three houses apart," I said.

"Hold on, three houses seems pretty far to throw a ball," T-Bone interrupted.

"Not in the city it isn't," I laughed. "Anyway the crack in the sidewalk was the base for each side. Two kids had a baseball glove and a tennis ball. Runners started on both ends. The two kids throwing would have a catch. The runners would try to get to the other side when the ball was thrown. You stayed in until you were tagged twice. Each tag was an out. The fewer the people, the more outs you were allowed. Last guy in won."

"That sounds like fun," said Wanda. "We should have games like that at the fair."

"What did you do when there was a funeral?" asked T-Bone. "Where did you play?"

"Out front or out back," I said. "Sometimes we would go out back and play Off the Wall."

"You would just bounce off the wall?" T-Bone gasped. "Didn't that hurt?"

"We didn't bounce ourselves off of the wall," I explained. "We would go in my yard and one guy would throw a tennis ball off the back of my house and one guy would go toward the back of the yard."

"How far back?" asked T-Bone. "Like the outfield in a baseball stadium?"

"Are you crazy?" I laughed. "It's a city yard, so it's narrow and about 30 feet long. Anyway, each fence post was a base. If the ball landed past the first post, it was a single, second post was a double, and third post was a triple. If you hit the green sandbox that rested up against the back fence it was a homerun. If the fielder caught the ball in the air or on one bounce, it was an out. The rest was like baseball."

"Okay, your mom and your grandparents let you throw a ball against the house?" Didn't it dent the siding?" he asked.

"It was a brick wall," I replied.

"And didn't the ball go in the neighbors' yards sometimes?" he asked.

"Yup," I said. "That's when we hopped the fences to get the ball. Before I moved in, what games did you play in New Jersey?"

"Well, we played baseball and um, I don't know," he thought. "Oh, we rode bikes, too. Did you?"

"Yeah, but it's a lot trickier riding in the city."

"We have to make lists of these games and keep them where kids will see them," said Wanda. "Like the illustrated snack list. We have to make sure kids know the importance of activity."

While T-Bone tried to do another pushup, Wanda and I started Googling community gardens. We immediately came across the *Greater Newark Conservancy*. Impressive didn't begin to describe this organization. The website said there was a program called Community Greening where they address the limited open spaces in Newark. They plant trees, landscape, enhance existing parks, plan community gardens, and create urban farms. They take vacant lots and help residents rent the lot for $1.00 per year. The Conservancy even offers assistance with seeds and workshops.

"That's brilliant," I said. "Absolutely brilliant."

"I agree," Wanda gushed. "They're ridding the city of the blight of vacant lots, using that space for something positive, providing healthy foods and teaching the residents skills."

"Hold on," I said as I kept reading. "They have urban farms in the state's biggest city and, as a result, they grow thousands of pounds of food. Then they have Youth Farm Stands where high school kids and college interns work, and they sell the produce to residents at very affordable prices. That's even more brilliant. This idea is perfect."

"Wait a minute," said Wanda. "They also have the Newark Youth Leadership Project, which provides mentorship, year-round training programs and exposure to outdoor activities."

"Hey Nick, I think perfect just got *perfecter*," T-Bone laughed.

"Not a word," Wanda corrected. "I think you meant to say *more perfect*."

"Nope," he said. "More perfect doesn't capture how perfect it is. Do you know what *perfecter* means?"

"It means you should've failed English?" she asked.

"No, it means beyond perfect," he nodded.

"You know what else means beyond perfect?" she asked. "*Beyond perfect*."

"Anyway," I interrupted, "we need to see how other communities are doing these things."

While Wanda scribbled more notes, I kept looking for more websites. A moment later, I stumbled on the *Healthy U* program, a partnership between the Horizon Foundation for New Jersey and the NJ YMCA State Alliance. It was designed to prevent childhood obesity by creating behavioral changes in kids ages 3–13. It teaches proper nutrition, how to increase moderate to vigorous physical activity, and motivates parents to get more involved with their kids to lead a healthier lifestyle. *Healthy U* even had its own curriculum called CATCH. The CATCH Program was designed for kids from pre-school through 8th grade. The idea was to teach kids that eating healthy and being physically active every day can be fun. CATCH has proven that healthy habits in childhood can create behavioral changes that can last a lifetime.

Wanda read it and said, "That's exactly what we're talking about. Preventing problems and not letting our generation be the generation that doesn't live as healthy or as long as our parents."

"How do they do it?" asked T-Bone. "With all of the commercials, the convenient food, the bright packages, and sugar snuck into almost everything, how do they do it?"

"Good question," said Wanda. "It says they start in preschool by nurturing a love of physical activity, classroom gardening, and healthy eating."

"No way," T-Bone protested. "That's so unfair."

"How is this unfair?" asked Wanda.

"I never got to be a farmer in pre-school," he replied. "We just sang, finger-painted and cried."

"Cried?" I asked. "You cried in pre-school?"

"Oh, sure," he said, "every day, buckets of tears."

"So, what happens after preschool?" I asked.

"Well," she read, "during school, healthy behaviors are reinforced in the classroom, the cafeteria and physical education class. Then they have after-school programs. In 2008, The Horizon Foundation and the New Jersey YMCA State Alliance created *Healthy U* and the program is in all of New Jersey's 21 counties."

"I know one thing," I said. "Ms. Swanson will be pretty impressed with everything we found."

"Definitely," Wanda and T-Bone said together.

By the time they left, we had found so many healthy things happening in New Jersey. Now, there was just one thing to do...ask my parents if we could take a really long day trip tomorrow.

Luckily, my parents were excited. I called Wanda and T-Bone and told them to meet at my house at 7:00 am. Since we enjoyed having kids who sent suggestions give us tours, Wanda reached out to Eden Collins. It was last-minute, but because she suggested Fosterfield Farms, we decided to see if she was available. Luckily, she was! After hanging up, I knew I had made a mistake, I should've told T-Bone and Wanda to meet at 8:00 am.

Chapter Nine

Old Mac T-Bone

The next morning, at exactly 6:00 am, our doorbell rang. Of course, we knew who it was. I stumbled down the steps, opened the front door and there they were. Even though I was half asleep, I wasn't too tired to see T-Bone's outfit. He was standing on my porch with rain boots, overalls, a thermal shirt under a plaid shirt, and he was wearing a big straw hat. Wanda was dressed normally and she just stood there, staring straight ahead. I figured she was trying to keep him out of her line of sight.

"Hey, Old Mac T-Bone, how's the farm'?" I asked.

"E-I-E-I-O," he laughed as he placed a stick in his mouth.

"And the stick?" I asked.

"Well, most farmers chew on some hay," he explained. "Since I don't have any, this will do."

"You don't think my mother is gonna let you ride around with a stick in your mouth, do you?"

"Hadn't thought of that pardner," he said, tipping his hat. "Could be a big problem, little doggie."

"Tell him farmers aren't cowboys," said Wanda.

"I would if I thought it would help," I laughed.

They came in and sat at the computer. Wanda said she needed to print a few more pages and check out a couple of things. T-Bone just sat there playing with straps on his overalls. By the time the rest of my family got ready and came downstairs, I could smell something cooking in the kitchen.

"What's going on?" I asked. "Aren't we supposed to be leaving right now?"

"Actually," said my mom, "I asked everyone to come over at 7:00 so we could eat a nice healthy breakfast before we got on the road. I have some eggs, turkey bacon, wheat toast, and fresh fruit."

"I'm in," said T-Bone. ·

"Mom, don't take this the wrong way," I said slowly as I scanned the kitchen, "but I've never seen you get up this early on a Sunday and start cooking."

"I know," she said as she blew the hair out of her eyes and filled a glass pitcher with ice water. "But it's gonna be a long day and I want to see if we can try to eat healthy all day. Wanda, you were right planning and organizing is the key."

"That's what the websites said," Wanda nodded. "It looks like they're right. Need help with anything?"

While my mom and Wanda went in the pantry, I started pouring ice water for everyone. My dad came down and took a glass without really looking and started drinking. Next, he started gagging.

"What happened to my orange juice?" he said, not expecting the ice water.

"I can answer that," said my mom. "Cold ice water is a nice alternative to juices and has no sugar."

"Oh, okay," my dad shrugged. "But, are we ever having orange juice again?" he asked.

"Of course, we'll have orange juice, again, but we have to not only factor food into the equation, but also beverages," she said. "People often overlook the sugar, calories, and carbs in drinks."

"Can I have chocolate milk?" asked Maggie. "And throw in some chocolate chips. Lots of them chips."

My mom didn't even answer her question. I was pretty sure our chocolate syrup was now at T-Bone's anyway. I handed Maggie her water and she seemed to enjoy it. Maybe it was the ice, maybe it was the fancy glass pitcher, whatever it was the water actually tasted great. Everyone ate their eggs, bacon, toast, and fruit and we cleaned up quickly. My mom and Wanda brought out a big cooler and asked me and my dad to put it in the back of the van. Before we carried it out, I looked inside. There were apples, individual peanut butter packages, cut-up vegetables, yogurt, a big container of tuna salad, a giant bowl with salad and my mom's homemade salad dressing.

"We're coming back tonight, right?" I joked. "It looks like enough food for a week."

"Very funny, wiseguy," she said as she patted my head. "It'll be a long day and we're eating dinner at The Brothers Moon, so we need to have enough food for eight people for all day. We can have a nice salad with some tuna salad on it for lunch, the rest can be for snacks."

"That looks awesome," said my dad as he gave her a kiss on the cheek. "Thanks, hon."

I suddenly realized what a good team my parents really were. I know some people might let the stress pull them apart, but my parents were closer. Actually the whole family, *including Wanda and T-Bone,* seemed closer. And now, when we all piled into van, we would be way closer.

We headed to some familiar roads, the New Jersey Turnpike and Interstate 287, on our way to Morristown. I was wondering why Wanda wasn't prepping everyone and then I realized how noisy the van was. When Maggie and Emma fell asleep, Wanda delivered her notes.

"Fosterfield Farms was once owned by General Joseph Warren Revere, the grandson of patriot Paul Revere," she began.

"Hold on," said T-Bone as he turned toward Wanda. "You mean, *the British are coming, the British are coming* Paul Revere?"

"Obviously," she said shaking her head. "Now in 1881, the farm was bought by Charles Foster and eventually given to the Morris County Park system in 1979 by Caroline Foster. Today, it represents farm life from 1880-1930."

"Is there fun stuff to do?" asked Timmy. "We're not just going to look at fruits and vegetables are we? Uh, no offense, Dad."

"None taken," my dad laughed.

"Actually, it's interactive," Wanda explained. "Kids churn butter, make cider, feed pigs, gather eggs and learn daily chores on this living history farm."

"Did you say chores?" asked Timmy. "I'm out. I'm not a big fan of chores. I have too many. I should have never asked my mom to teach me how to do laundry. I talked myself right into having a chore."

"Everyone has to help out," said my mom, realizing Timmy was on to her. She had been telling him he was the best laundry guy ever, and that worked for a while. Now, he realized laundry was a chore. My mom, as usual, was one step ahead of him. When Timmy said he wanted to quit being the laundry guy, she told him he was right.

"I am?" he asked. "Really?"

"Of course you are," she said. "I've taken terrible advantage and didn't realize it. You're, by far the best laundry guy in the house.You shouldn't be called laundry guy. You need a really fancy title."

"I do?" he asked.

"Of course, you do," she confirmed. "But we can't just go giving titles away, willy-nilly, right?"

"I don't think so," he said, slowly being lured into her trap. He was like those little bugs who see a spider web and think, *that looks pretty*. She whispered something in my dad's ear and looked back at Timmy. Then, as she was about to speak, she whispered to my dad once more. Finally, she looked at Timmy and said, "We've never done this before, not even for Nicky, but we are promoting you. From now on, your title is *Laundry Master.*"

"No way," he said. "Seriously? Laundry Master? I always wanted to master something. Awesome."

"You deserve it," my mom said with a wink.

"Hey, is it okay if I do the laundry sometimes?" asked my dad, totally testing my mom's work.

"Sorry, Dad," Timmy shook his head. "But you're not a Laundry Master. You better leave it to me."

Once again my mom's work was impeccable. Wanda looked at me in amazement. I wasn't as surprised since I was once the Garbage Master, the Broom Master, and the Pick-up Toys Master.

"Take notes about that," I whispered to Wanda. "That could come in handy one day."

"You mean when I'm a parent?" she asked.

"Sure," I laughed, "but I was thinking of T-Bone."

"Back to the pre-trip details," said T-Bone.

"So," said Wanda, "Spring's a good time to visit because the garden's being prepared for planting and weekends are more active with costumed volunteers to bring the experience to life."

"Do they have special events?" asked my mom.

"Yes," Wanda read. "They have active festivals that are fully staffed and are held periodically throughout the year. Farm animals can be seen and interacted with, like pigs, chickens, a lamb, horses and cows. At times, the cows can be milked."

"I'm so excited," my mom gushed as we pulled up.

We woke up my sisters, piled out of the van and smelled that fresh clean air. It was a sunny day and the farm looked awesome. The volunteers were really dressed in the clothes from that time period and as T-Bone would probably say at some point, *this was another New Jersey time machine.*

Just as we started heading over, my dad said, "Wait here, everyone, I forgot something."

He came back with a small bag, opened it up and started handing something out to everyone.

"What's this, Mr. A.?" asked Wanda.

"That is a pedometer," my dad proudly announced.

"Wanda, tell your mom she doesn't need to buy you one. This one is on me. Guys, place these lanyards around your neck and it will count your steps."

"No way!" said T-Bone. "You really bought these for all of us? That must have been some coupon."

"Nope," my dad shook his head. "No coupon."

"Were they giving them away free?" he continued.

"No, Tommy," my sad sighed, "I bought them for everyone."

"I don't believe it," he said. "Not you."

There it was. My dad had been so calm since his diagnosis that I started worrying about him. But he was back to his old frustrated-at-T-Bone self.

"Just put it on," he said as he handed out the rest. My mom said we would all start tracking our steps and how long we were sleeping, as well as any other activities, using Wanda's tracking sheets.

"Hey, it even has the time," T-Bone announced. "Don't forget, Mr. A., two hours until lunch."

"Don't worry, it's all coming back to me," said my dad as he shook his head.

We met up with Eden, and her family, at the Visitors Center. She was with her parents, Jonathan and Jill, and her little sister, Anabel. They told us they lived so close that they visited the farm frequently, mostly for the animals.

"Hi, everyone," my mom said, leading the way. She introduced all of us, even though I was sure poor Eden's family would never remember our names.

It took all of four-seconds for both families to start talking like we had been friends forever. Maggie and Emma wanted to hold Anabel's hands when she walked. My mom and Jill started comparing kid stories and my dad and Jonathan compared the fastest ways to get around New Jersey.

Wanda immediately walked over to Eden. She was a fourth grader at Normandy Park School in Morristown. From the moment we met her,until we said good-bye, she never stopped smiling. In fact, my mother told her three times that she had a beautiful smile.

"So, Eden, tell us about yourself," said Wanda.

"What do you wanna know," she asked.

"Anything," said Wanda, not realizing that it could be hard to just start talking about yourself.

"Well," I said, trying to help her out, "how about I give you some questions?"

"Sure," she nodded.

"Okay, maybe you can tell us your favorite food, favorite color, favorite activities," I suggested. "Things like that."

"Oh, that's easy," she said. "I love pickles, light green, gymnastics, art, winter, chocolate ice cream, drawing, reading, swimming, and Asbury Park."

"Well, that was easy," I laughed.

"Eden, we're trying to get kids to be healthier while they're still kids so they can stay healthy for life," said Wanda. "Do you mind if we add you to our sample and ask you some questions?"

"I don't know what that means," she said with a smile, "but sure."

"Well, we're trying to figure out what people know and how they feel about being healthy," Wanda explained. "The people we ask are our sample group, so you would be a sample. Is that okay?"

"Everyone loves free samples, so sure," she said.

"That's exactly what I said when they made me a sample," exclaimed T-Bone.

Poor Eden, I thought. She's thinking like T-Bone!

"So, Eden," Wanda continued, "what types of things do you do to stay healthy?"

"Well, I eat a vegetable at every meal and my favorite snack is carrots and hummus," she said.

"I love carrots and hummus, too," Wanda agreed.

"I'm also very, very active," she said. "I really love gymnastics, running, and kayaking."

"Okay, which one would you rather do, exercise or activities?" I asked.

"Definitely activities," she said without hesitation. "Exercise sounds boring, but activities are fun."

We all agreed and we were ready to explore. On Eden's advice, we toured the 1920's farmhouse, where the farm foreman lived. We saw farmers in a wagon, pulled by the biggest horses I'd ever seen, and then the mansion. We learned that Paul Revere's grandson, Gen. Joseph Warren Revere, built the mansion called *The Willows*. I wondered how big a house had to be to get a name. When the Foster Family bought the property in 1881 they changed the name to Fosterfields. Caroline Foster lived 98 of her 102 years in that mansion. I wanted to tour the mansion and see the inside, but all of the sisters wanted to see animals. To avoid buckets of tears, we compromised. Animals first, followed by the mansion tour.

"Caroline Foster was a pretty lucky kid," said T-Bone.

"You mean lucky person," I corrected, "she lived in this awesome mansion for 98-years."

"You mean generous person," said Wanda. "It's only because of her generosity, and desire to have future generations understand what her era was like, that we're here today."

"True," said T-Bone. "If she wasn't so generous, we'd be trespassing right now."

We walked all around the property and even spoke to the costumed interpreters. They were really knowledgeable and helpful. We decided we'd return for the festivals, especially the 1920 County Fair. Eden's family said they'd meet us there.

We walked around the farm, fed the chickens and even read about the history. Eden and her family were great and Anabel didn't want to let go of my sisters' hands. We thanked them for the suggestion and the tour and told Eden we would be in touch.

When we returned to the car, we all checked our pedometers. Most of us were at about 4,000 steps. I could see this starting to get very competitive.

It was a little after noon, so my mom took out the cooler and plates. She plated the salads and topped them with some dressing and tuna salad as Wanda passed them out.

"No, thanks," said T-Bone, "One burger, please."

"T-Bone," said Wanda, *giving him the eye.* "This is lunch. At a farm. Outside. It's like a picnic."

"Salad isn't the first course?" he whispered.

"No, it's not the first course," she said, staring at him even harder. "This is lunch. Where do you think a burger would come from? Do you see a grill? Do you think this is a magical hot cooler?"

"Do they make hot coolers?" he asked, clearly not understanding her obvious body language.

"Why would they call something hot, a cooler?" she asked. "Now, are you taking this salad?"

"Sure," he said, looking a little afraid of Wanda.

As it turned out, lunch was fantastic. Everyone complimented my mom, even T-Bone. When we cleaned up, we headed south to the Duke Farms.

The ride to the Duke Farms was pretty quick, well, compared to the ride to Fosterfields Farm from our house. While we drove, Wanda read the three suggestions from Fiona, Alex, and Briana, as well as some research she had printed. It was clear that this place would be beautiful.

Wanda told us that the Duke Family was very wealthy and that they owned the American Tobacco Company.

"Hold on," said T-Bone. "We're going to a place that makes cigarettes? That's crazy? I'm not a doctor, but even I know they kill people."

"T-Bone, they don't make cigarettes, now," said Wanda. "That was a long time ago; way before people knew cigarettes were bad."

"Burnt toast is bad," said T-Bone. "Getting splashed by a bus is bad. Smoking isn't just bad, SMOKING WILL KILL YOU."

"Tommy, history buffs respect the differences between eras," my mom quietly explained, trying to calm him down. "Each generation evolves, or they should. You can't judge previous generations based upon what you know *now,* that they didn't know *then.*"

"I guess," he said.

"Think of it this way," said Wanda, "a hundred years from now, kids might judge us for doing foolish things that we never knew were foolish."

"Like using multiple names for sugar and labeling our food in metric?" he asked.

"Actually, yes," Wanda continued. "So anyway, the Duke Farms is truly an amazing example of environmental stewardship."

"That's what Karen, from DEP, said when we met her at Ringwood State Park, remember?" I asked.

"Oh, yeah," said T-Bone. "She said that the people of the Department of Environmental Protection were stewards of the environment."

"Exactly," said Wanda. "The Duke Family also serves as stewards. Their website says they are on 2,740 acres in Hillsborough, Somerset County, N.J., and are one of the largest privately-owned parcels of undeveloped land in the state. Owned and supported by Duke Farms Foundation, an operating foundation of the Doris Duke Charitable Foundation, Duke Farms is rich in ecological, horticultural and agricultural resources."

"Who's Doris Duke?" asked Timmy.

"She was the only daughter of James Duke. He died, in 1925, when she was twelve years old and she was his sole heir," said Wanda, paging through her notes. "The newspapers called her the richest little girl in America."

"I bet they were very philanthropic," I said, knowing how T-Bone wanted to be a philanthropist and donate money to good causes one day.

"They were very philanthropic," said Wanda. "In Durham, North Carolina, Trinity College became Duke University after the Duke Family's $40 million donation. When she died back in 1993, the Doris Duke Charitable Foundation was worth an estimated $1.2 billion.

"1.2 billion dollars?" shrieked T-Bone. "Billion with a 'B'?"

"That's a lot of money," I said, shaking my head.

"I looked at the pictures and, just the orientation center, which was an old barn, looks unbelievable," said Wanda. "Oh, and they have a farm-to-table program from May through November so people can buy fresh produce and unique products."

"I wonder why she didn't sell it?" I asked.

"Well, she had other huge estates in places like Hawaii, Los Angeles, and New York," said Wanda. "I think she wanted to continue her father's legacy. Their site says, through the beauty of its natural setting, the diversity of its wildlife, and the scope and quality of its educational programs, research and demonstrations, Duke Farms inspires people to transform their approach to conservation and to start building a more sustainable future."

"I thought I heard once that they have some solar panels," said my dad.

"They do," said Wanda. "They have over 3,000 solar panels, which is enough to power the entire estate, 100%."

"Do they have tours? Do they have a gift shop?" asked T-Bone.

"They don't have tours, they don't have a gift shop, and you can't go inside the mansion," Wanda read from her notes. "They have a cafe, lots of trails, and places to relax."

Just as she finished her sentence, we arrived. It was as impressive as I expected. The grounds were unbelievable and the Orientation Center was massive. They had one of the things I really enjoy, which was a short film. I was always so interested to see what the real people looked like. Home movies were always my favorite as people were usually much more casual and relaxed.

We learned that the farm was very serious about protecting the environment and resources. Great stewardship, I thought. There were electric cars that the employees drove around the estate and they even had their own charging stations. There was a bus stop, right by the gate, to encourage people to use public transportation. Very well-planned, I thought.

"You'll love this," said Wanda, "the Duke Farms Urban Agriculture Regional Training Center."

"That's awesome," said T-Bone. "What is it?"

"They teach people how to bring agriculture into urban areas. And they even rent plots of land for local gardeners," said Wanda.

"That's pretty generous," I said.

"Because of demand," Wanda continued, "there are up to 462 plots and the rent is a very reasonable

$20-$60 depending upon the size. It must be real popular because the website says they're sold out."

"I love that they're working to bring fresh produce to everyone," my dad commented.

We did love it. We learned that they were at the forefront of bringing very important issues to the public, but even better, they show people how to do these things. From time to time, we would stop and sit under a tree to take it all in. Happily, we also got our steps in; this time, we added 6,000 steps. The best part, no one realized we had walked so much because we were having fun.

As we headed out, we agreed to return soon, next time with our bikes. Luckily, the fresh air wiped my sisters out and they happily jumped into the van. Within three minutes, both were sound asleep. Our final destination would be in Hopewell Township and The Brothers Moon. We read great things about it and Wanda had checked it out online. It sounded great; farm-to-table foods. She read some of the information she had found: "Opened in Hopewell Borough on the main street in 2000, they were the first "Farm-to-Table" restaurant in the area. The Brothers Moon is an 80-100 seat full-service restaurant featuring a seasonally changing menu with daily additions.

The beautiful front patio offers seasonal al fresco dining, in the heart of pretty Hopewell Borough. We pledge to use the finest ingredients in all that we prepare for our customers."

"Sounds good to me," I said.

Luckily, from Hillsborough, it didn't take long to get there and it was right on Main Street. We sat outside and the server immediately brought over some ice water. I was shocked, but I was getting used to drinking ice water. It actually tasted good; in fact, the colder the better. We looked over the menu and everything sounded great.

While my parents had chicken and vegetable dinners, all of the kids ordered a cheeseburger. I wasn't sure why, but the burger was amazing. If it wasn't enough reason to give up fast food burgers, nothing was. The flavor was great and even my sisters noticed. They shared a burger and still wanted more. Sarah Miller Piotrowski definitely knew what she was talking about when she happily recommended this restaurant.

We spoke to the chef and told him about our day and he said he was happy we could stop in. He also told us to consider visiting Hopewell for future trips because of the town's rich history and nature.

We told him that when we did return, we would be coming back to see him, and he said he would look forward to it.

As usual, it truly was a *Garden State Adventure*. Thanks to the suggestions from so many amazing New Jersey kids, we were able to explore some of New Jersey's most beautiful, natural, and historic sites... *while we collected thousands of steps.*

Chapter Ten

Mr. Frog on a Log

The next day, we were exhausted. We had topped 12,000 steps, which was almost 6 miles. It was no wonder my sisters had fallen asleep in the car. Ms. Swanson had asked us to bring our lunch to her office to discuss the fair and pre-fair activities. She apologized for the delay in distributing our survey and told us it would go out the next morning.

A moment later, Mr. B. and Mr. J., two of our gym teachers, arrived, followed by the nurse, Mrs. Leary. They were very excited about the fair and loved our idea about the name change. They agreed that the key element of wellness had to be keeping the necessary steps fun and positive.

As Wanda took notes, I told them about the *Austin the Unstoppable* program and they were all very interested. Ms. Swanson said she would run it by the administration and see if they were available. We decided that if they were, they would be a great kickoff activity to start the wellness conversation. I was sure that when kids saw how many teaspoons of sugar were in things like soda, it would make them think twice. At least, I hoped it would.

Mr. B asked us if we had thought about any New Jersey role models and suggested a PGA golfer named Morgan Hoffman. He told us that Morgan was a true athlete, working out every day, eating healthy, and maintaining a sleep schedule.

"Do you have to work out to play golf?" asked T-Bone. "I thought it was just old, rich guys."

Mr. B and Mr. J. both laughed. I only watched golf when my dad had it on, but even I knew that there were amazing young golfers and women golfers. While you didn't need to work out for golf, I figured it must help if you're playing on the PGA tour.

"He's a native of Bergen County, NJ, and he wears a pedometer to track his steps," said Mr. B. "He even raised money with Healthy Steps NJ by tracking his steps."

We all held up our pedometers at the same time.

"Not only does he track steps," said Mr. B., "He packs healthy lunches to control what he's eating."

"That's really smart," said Wanda. "We just learned that one of the reasons obesity rates are so high is because people eat outside of the home so much more. If a golfer is on tour, he's probably not home much and that could become a problem."

"Exactly," said Mrs. Leary. "It's hard enough to eat healthy when you are home. That must be some challenge when you're on the road frequently. For starters, you can't control the ingredients and then, of course, there's the portion sizes."

"We read about that, too," said T-Bone. "And, we also read that people have become less active."

"Very true," said Mr. J. "That's also a problem."

"Do you think if we e-mailed him some questions, he would reply?" I asked.

All of the teachers looked at each other and agreed that it could never hurt to try. They even offered to find an address. I decided that we would ask him to share his best tips and advice. As a real professional golfer, his words would be well-received. *If he wrote back, that is.* Being on tour, I had no idea how often he checked his mail.

"So how do we approach this?" asked Wanda.

Ms. Swanson said we should look at the answers to the questionnaires first. Once we knew what was confusing kids, we could brainstorm.

Everyone agreed and Mr. B. asked us to think about two other issues. The first was asthma. As a physical education teacher, he was concerned that many kids with asthma limit their activity needlessly and avoid strenuous activities. He told us about the BEAM program, an initiative between the Horizon Foundation of New Jersey and the Boys & Girls Clubs in New Jersey.

"Oh, is that a gymnastics program for kids with asthma?" asked T-Bone.

"What?" Mr. B. asked, suddenly confused.

"You said beam," said T-Bone. "There's a beam you balance on in gymnastics. I can't think of the name, right now, but you balance on this beam."

"A balance beam," I sighed.

"Yes, that's what you do," he insisted. "It's in the Olympics. You must've seen it before. A thin beam that you balance on."

"That's called a balance beam," Wanda yelled, shocking everyone. "I'm sorry, but sometimes I can't take it anymore. T-Bone, it's called a balance beam *and that's also what you do on it.*"

"Oh," T-Bone shrugged. "You don't have to yell."

"Kinda do," she said, still shaking her head.

"Anyway," Mr. B. continued, "it stands for Breathe Easier with Asthma Management and it was designed to help kids manage asthma instead of letting asthma manage them."

"What a positive approach," Wanda said, regaining her composure. "It's like focusing on being healthy instead of dieting; it's all about positive attitude."

"Exactly," Mr. B. nodded. "Taking control of your own health is so much more effective. It's just like Ben Franklin said."

"Don't fly a kite in a storm?" asked Mrs. Leary.

"No," Mr. B. smiled.

"Well done is better than well said?" asked Ms. Swanson.

"No, but that is one of my favorites," he agreed.

"William Franklin, you join this revolution right now or you're punished," guessed T-Bone.

"Funny," he said, "but no. Since Ben Franklin probably has a thousand expressions, let me just tell you. An ounce of prevention..."

"Ooh, I know this one. A teaspoon, no a tablespoon, no wait, an ounce of prevention is worth a liter of cure," T-Bone shouted, then corrected himself. "No wait, a meter, wait, it's on the tip of my tongue."

"Pound," Wanda yelled again, "it's a pound."

"So you were telling us about the BEAM program," I reminded him.

"Oh, yeah, I almost forgot," he laughed. "So the idea is to provide kids, parents, and caregivers with the tools to manage asthma."

"I know a lot of kids have asthma," I said, "but what is it exactly?"

"Well, it's a disorder that causes the airways in the lungs to swell and become narrow," said Mrs. Leary. "It's one of the most common recurring childhood illnesses. The good news is that asthma attacks can be prevented and managed and when that happens, kids can lead normal, healthy lives."

"How do you know if you have it?" I asked.

"The most common symptoms are coughing, wheezing, shortness of breath, and tightness in your chest," she explained. "The triggers can be tobacco smoke, dust mites, outdoor air pollution, pets, and mold."

"Speaking as a gym teacher," said Mr. B., "we never want to see a kid afraid to play, or afraid to play hard, because of asthma. That's why the BEAM program is so important."

As we discussed helping kids with asthma, something I never would have thought of on my own, I realized why committees work. Everyone brings something different to the conversation. That's something we would have never thought about.

His second issue was something he had seen last season at a Somerset Patriots Minor League baseball game. It was called *Healthy Plate*.

"I've heard of healthy food," said T-Bone, "but never a *healthy plate*. Are people so hungry that when they're done, they have room for the plate? And what's it made of?"

"It's not a plate that you eat," Mr. J. laughed. "It's a plate containing healthy foods."

"Oh, that was my second guess," said T-Bone.

"Well, sports venues are notorious for unhealthy foods," said Mrs. Leary. "It almost a tradition to go to a game and get a hot dog, soda, or ice cream."

"Exactly," said Mr. J., "and that's mostly because that's the only food you can buy. It seems like every venue has tons of stands that sell hog dogs, pizza, nachos, pretzels, and candy. But the *Healthy Plate* concession offers healthy options, like a grilled chicken sandwich, salad, and a turkey burger. Plus, they use Jersey Fresh menu items."

"I wonder what made them decide to do that," I asked. "I would have guessed that the healthy food stand wouldn't have a long line."

"They actually did a survey a few years ago and families wanted healthier options and more choices," he said.

"That's hopeful," said Wanda.

"I read an article that Steve Kalafer, the owner of the Patriots, completely supported it," said Mr. B. "Now, the Lakewood Blue Claws and the Trenton Thunder have Healthy Plate concessions. The New York Red Bulls have it, too."

"I have a question," said Wanda. "Is it overpriced? Because sometimes parents have to pick the $2.00 hot dog over the $10.00 healthy sandwich."

"Nope," said Mr. J., "the food's affordable and they give you the calorie count. They also offer things like baked potatoes, broccoli, fruits, vegetarian chili, sugar-free water ice and gluten free cookies."

"If you kids write about this and spread the word," said Ms. Swanson, "more people may try it. The more people that go, the more *Healthy Plate* concessions we'll see popping up."

"And even better than that," said Mrs. Leary, "it might result in people changing the way they eat."

"Even though it's healthier, would that be bad for fast food and convenience food companies? Would they go out of business and have people lose their jobs?" I wondered.

"Actually, being able to adapt is the sign of a good business," said Mr. J. "If consumers demand healthier options, fast food and convenience food companies would change their menus."

"We'd have a lot less food-related problems than countries without enough food," said Wanda.

"She raises a good point," said Mr. B., "with all of our technology and information, combined with an abundance of food choices, as a society, we're kind of a disaster. I mean a real mess."

We told them about the things we had learned recently, especially the awesome Greater Newark Conservancy and the Duke Farms. They agreed that we needed to do more to affordably bring fresh produce to urban areas.

Mr. J. and Mr. B. asked if we had suggestions for fun activities and we told them about Pop's games. They loved the ideas and said they played those games when they were kids. They even had ideas.

"I would like to see kids jumping rope," said Mr. B., "and also, hula hooping."

"I'm good with hula hooping," said T-Bone, "but can we cross off jumping rope?"

Everyone turned, confused, and looked at T-Bone.

"What?" he said. "I don't think it's a very physical activity, so let's just cross it off."

"Tommy, it's actually very physical," said Mr. B.

"Well, then," he thought for a moment, "it's a major tripping hazard. "It's a very dangerous activity."

Mr. J. started laughing. "Are you seriously calling jump rope a dangerous activity?"

"For the record, it can be very dangerous," he insisted. "Those jump ropes might look innocent, but you could trip, fall, get rope burns, and hit yourself in the head with the wooden handles. You could even poke your eye out."

"Tommy, that's the most ridiculous thing I've ever heard," said Ms. Swanson. "Little kids jump rope. What's really going on?"

"Nothing," he said very defensively. "Nothing at all. I'm just worried about the safety and well-being of my classmates. Would I *really* be a good Co-president if I just allowed my classmates to endanger their lives with a jump rope?"

The room fell silent. No one quite knew what to say. Finally, Ms. Swanson spoke.

"Tommy," she said slowly, "let me ask you one question. Do you know how to jump rope?"

"Okay, okay," he said standing up and rubbing his head as if he were confessing to a crime. I wished I had a video camera ready to go. "Congratulations. You figured it out. I can't jump rope. I've tried a million times. I see those little kids do it without even thinking about it. But I just can't do it. Trust me, it is impossible to teach me to jump rope."

I looked around the room and realized why everyone was looking away. They were trying not to laugh. That is, except Wanda, who was staring at him, wide-eyed. Wow, I thought to myself. You think you know a guy and then you find out that a guy who can speak comfortably in front of a thousand people, can't jump over a length of rope.

"Tommy, you need to relax," said Mr. J. "Anyone can learn to jump rope. I've never met a person who tried, that couldn't figure it out. Did you accidentally try to jump Double Dutch? You know, with two ropes twirling at the same time?"

"No," he said. "One me, one rope, and one video."

"*A video?*" Mrs. Leary asked, trying not to laugh.

"Yeah," he mumbled, staring at the floor. "It was called *Jumping Rope with Mr. Frog on a Log.*"

"Mr. Frog?" asked Ms. Swanson, her eyes filling up and her face turning a very bright shade of red.

"Yeah, Mr. Frog, Your Pal On The Log, promised he could teach any kid to jump rope," he nodded. "They ended up giving my mom her money back."

At that point, Mr. B. and Mr. J. stood up and ran out of the office, leaving poor Ms. Swanson and Mrs. Leary to hold in their laughter. Wanda, on the other hand, still hadn't blinked. She couldn't believe that T-Bone couldn't jump rope.

A few moments later, Mr. B and Mr. J. returned, more composed and carrying a jump rope. Oh no, I thought, not in front of Wanda. As much as I was enjoying this strange turn of events, I felt like I needed to save my friend.

"Can I borrow that rope and teach T-Bone at home?" I asked.

"Sure," they said, "but if you need a hand, holler."

I couldn't believe it. I was now a jump rope tutor. Poor T-Bone! The only thing that would've been worse is if they said to drop and give them ten!

"Before we wrap up," said Ms. Swanson, "there were two other things I wanted to discuss. The first is adding an international flair to the fair."

"Flair to the fair?" I asked.

"Yes," she said. "I have a friend who teaches at Mount Prospect School in Basking Ridge and they host an International Day each year. It's an elaborate event, and because the students in that school hail from dozens of countries, they have a lot of firsthand expertise."

"Are you thinking about incorporating healthy foods from different cultures?" asked Wanda.

"Exactly," she smiled. "We don't have the same levels of diversity here, but that shouldn't stop us. So many other countries don't experience the same issues we experience, so maybe we should see what they're doing."

"Sounds like a great idea," said Mrs. Leary. "In this day and age, it's important to start teaching our children about other cultures. It really is a small world and there's so much to learn from others."

"You said you had two issues, Ms. Swanson," I reminded her.

"That's right. Are you familiar with *Celebrate New Jersey*? They have creative, educational programs that excite and inspire New Jersey students," she explained.

"I've heard of it," I said.

"Well, they have some amazing programs," she continued. "And they work really hard to promote New Jersey, so your work is very similar."

"I love anything that supports New Jersey," I said.

"And they used to have a program called CRUNCH BUNCH," she smiled. "The website says childhood obesity is a growing epidemic in the United States. Although it's a complex issue, many experts agree that educating children about the importance of healthy food choices and physical activity, early in life, can play a powerful role in preventing obesity and its consequences. Children may also become *change-agents* for their families just by sharing information about healthy living at home."

"I love the part about children being change agents," said Wanda. "That's brilliant."

"They believe," read Ms. Swanson, "that learning's better when it's fun, and in engaging kids in things like creative writing, poems, stories, skits, songs, etc. on the theme of healthy living, nutrition, safety, wellness, and choices to create lasting impact over the course of their lifetimes."

"Yes!" said T-Bone. "Learning works better when it's fun. I love this program. Can I write a poem and send it in?"

"Sadly, the program was discontinued," she explained. "But I did meet the Executive Director, Heather Tedesco, at an event and maybe you can reach out to her to discuss bringing it back or using some of its elements. She's a wonderful person."

"That's brilliant," said Wanda, "it's fun, creative and it'll make a difference. I love it."

"Hold on," I said. "Before everyone gets too excited, we don't even know if she'd want to do it with us."

"Can't hurt to ask," said Mrs. Leary.

"Okay, I think we covered everything, folks," said

Ms. Swanson. "Let's break for now and meet in a couple of days to review the questionnaires."

"Okay," we all said at the same time.

As we left, Mr. B. whispered, "Seriously, if you need help teaching him to jump rope, let me know."

"Will do," I said, holding the rope. "How hard can it really be?"

"I don't know," he said, "ask Mr. Frog on a Log."

That night, at dinner, I told my parents about our meeting. They said it sounded like the most productive meeting, ever. Not having been to many meetings in my life, I had to take their word for it. They loved everything I told them. My mom thought the Horizon Foundation's Healthy U and Healthy Plate initiative was genius and she loved the BEAM program. My dad actually knew who Morgan Hoffman was and watched him on the PGA tour. He said he was a great athlete and known for living a clean, healthy life.

When I told my mom about the International Flair at the Fair, she loved the idea and hoped she could get some good ideas for our family. I also asked her if she knew about *Celebrate New Jersey* and the

CRUNCH BUNCH. She had read about it and knew it was a popular program. She even noticed the similarities with us.

"There was one other thing," I told them. "Would you believe T-Bone can't jump rope?"

"What do you mean?" asked my dad. "Everybody can jump rope; unless you're trying to do Double Dutch, of course. That's a little trickier."

"Nope," I laughed. "Just plain old jump rope, like Maggie and Emma do."

"Okay, then I have a question," said my dad. "Why did *you* bring home a jump rope?"

"That's the best part of the whole day," I laughed. "I'm gonna be T-Bone's jump rope tutor."

My parents both had the same frozen, wide-eyed look that Wanda had in Ms. Swanson's office. Finally, my dad spoke. "Can we watch?"

The next day, Ms. Swanson had the questionnaires passed out and collected during first period. The school secretaries volunteered to tally the answers so we would know what was confusing everyone. *It turned out everything was*. Wanda said that was a good news-bad news situation. The good news was that we knew what we had to explain. The bad news was that it was everything.

By the end of the week, we had two more lunch meetings with the teachers and some kids who had volunteered to share foods from their cultures. Besides healthy American foods, we now had foods from Italy, Mexico, India, China, and Jamaica.

T-Bone volunteered his mom without even asking her. Luckily she agreed to make big batches of Garden Minestrone soup.

Rosa Diaz offered to have her mom make trays of Sweet Potato and Spinach Quesadillas. She said they were nutritious and delicious. Ms. Swanson said her mouth was already watering. Mrs. Diaz even offered to cut them into small pieces.

Sahara Patel's mom said she would make Tandori Chicken Bites. She cooks them with yogurt and they're low carb-high protein. Sahara said her mom was a good cook, making healthy food taste great.

Marlon Harris said his dad would prepare several trays of Jamaican Grilled Chicken and Pineapple. He said it was one of his dad's best dishes. It was healthy, a little sweet, and loaded with protein. Matthew Kim's parents offered to make a few trays of steamed chicken with snow peas. I couldn't remember if I had ever eaten steamed chicken, but it sounded healthier than fried. Mrs. Kim would also cut the pieces small so kids could sample it.

The rest of us volunteered to bring healthy choices. I was bringing healthy cereals and low-fat milk. Wanda was bringing cut up vegetables with a low-fat dip. Even teachers were bringing healthy dishes. This Fun Fit Fair with International Flair was really shaping up.

The fair was in a few weeks, which wasn't a lot of time. We made a floor plan of the gym, as well as where tables and activities would go. Mr. B. and Mr. J. came in handy since it was their classroom.

A committee of students that made charts and posters to advertise the fair. The whole school started tracking sleep, steps, and activities. The school was buzzing with excitement. Just when I thought it couldn't get any better, Ms. Swanson delivered the best news yet. The *Austin the Unstoppable* show was available to come to our school on Monday. I couldn't believe it.

Wanda and I checked our to-do list and it seemed

like everything was falling into place. We needed to wrap up a few details, but compared to what we had already done, that was minor. Plus, we had a lot of help. As prepared as we were, I kept getting the feeling that I was forgetting something. As hard as I tried, I just could not remember what it was. Then I went home, walked in my room, and there it was, sitting on my desk...the jump rope.

Besides the jump rope, there was something else waiting for us...a letter from Morgan Hoffman, the New Jersey golfer on the PGA tour. I couldn't believe he wrote back. I immediately called T-Bone and got as far as, "You know Morgan Hoffman?"

A moment later, he was standing behind me. "Is he here? Did he call? Was there an e-mail? Is he on his way? Is the media coming, too? How's my hair look? What's my better side? You know you can't just call and leave me hanging like that."

"Leave you hanging?" I said. "That's a good one! I said six words and you hung up."

"What's going on?" he continued. "Wanda here?"

"I called Wanda after you hung up. She's on her way," I confirmed. "And yup, we got a letter."

Wanda came in and we slowly slid the letter out of the crisp white envelope with my name and address handwritten in black ink. It looked so official. When I opened it up, I was even more impressed. It was a handwritten note.

Dear Nicky, T-Bone, and Wanda,

Thanks for reaching out to me and for your efforts to promote health and wellness. To answer some of your questions, I was born in Englewood, NJ and I grew up in Wyckoff and Franklin Lakes. Except for finishing high school at a golf academy, in South Carolina and Florida, I have lived in the Garden State my whole life. I started swinging a golf club when I was in diapers and entered my first golf tournament when I was eight years old.

Now, being a professional athlete requires many things, like dedication. Growing up, I was on the golf range every day, except when I played hockey and baseball. Today, when I have a week off from the tour, I practice six hours a day. I know that must sound like a lot, and it is very tedious, but I love getting better and challenging myself. Now as far as being healthy, that's very important to me. I am really strict with my diet. I don't eat any dairy, any fried foods, and I'm leaning off gluten. I work out 4 days a week and on my off days I do stretch-

ing and metabolic exercises. If you're not sure what that is, they're fast-pace-exercises to get your heart rate high. My trainer, Don Saladino, is amazing. Now, besides eating healthy and being active, I am a huge fan of sleep. I make sleep a priority and get 8-hours every night. Of course, being on tour, I travel a lot, so I'm dedicated to being as healthy as possible, even on the road. Golf is an amazing, challenging sport and I would love to see more kids get involved.

My advice to any future golfers would be to take advantage of New Jersey's summer's weather, then find a great coach or teacher for the winter. No matter what, whether you want to be a golfer or not, always focus on making good choices.
I hope that helps!

Best wishes,
Morgan Hoffman

"Nick, did you hear that? Did you hear that?" said T-Bone, his heart racing.

"Obviously," I laughed. "I just read it out loud."

"We should figure out a way to include his advice at the fair," said Wanda.

201

"And we should add golf to our list of activities," said T-Bone.

"Add golf?" I shrieked. "You know golf is 18-holes?"

"I know we can't do all of the holes," he answered. "But we can do one hole."

"You have watched golf , right?" Wanda wondered.

"Watch? No. Play? A lot," he replied.

"When have you ever golfed?" I asked.

"On our day trips," he said. "Remember, playing golf at Bill Burr's on Long Beach Island?"

"Hold on," I said, looking at Wanda. "T-Bone, do you think Morgan is a professional mini-golfer?"

"Obviously," he said with a smirk. "That's why we should have one golf hole in the gym. Let's get the one with a windmill; it's so hard. When you get the ball past the blade and sink it, it's exhilarating. But, I'm open to debate. If you want to do something with an alligator's mouth or a secret passage that leads to the cup, I'm cool with that. I just wish Morgan would have told us his favorite."

"Let me," Wanda sighed. "T-Bone, Morgan isn't a professional mini-golfer. He plays real golf, on a golf course. He has a golf bag with lots of golf clubs and a caddy, not a green or red ball and a putter."

"What?" he gasped. "He's one of those guys you see on TV? We got a letter from a TV golf guy?"

"Yup," we both answered together.

T-Bone was shocked. This whole time he thought Morgan was on some imaginary pro-mini-golf tour. He must have re-read the letter twenty times. With T-Bone busy re-reading, Wanda had an idea. While we couldn't fit a golf hole in the gym, and we didn't have access to a mini-golf hole, we could still include golf. Wanda's dad had an indoor putter mat. She said that you unroll the green rug and try to putt the ball up the hill and in the cup.

"Hi kids," a voice from the kitchen hollered.

"Pop?" I hollered back.

"What are you up to?" he asked as he came in.

"Planning the Fit Fun Fair," I replied. "We just got a letter from Morgan Hoffman."

"The PGA golfer?" asked Pop.

"Yes!" exclaimed T-Bone. "And he plays real golf, not mini-golf. He even has more than one club."
"You don't say," Pop pretended to be surprised. "I read an article that said he's also a pilot who some-times flies his own plane to his golf tournaments."

"What?" T-Bone exclaimed. "I'm holding a real letter from a professional golfer and pilot?"

"Appears so," Pop smiled. "So do you kids have a lot of homework this weekend?"

We weren't sure why he was asking, but it turned out he was taking a ride to Tuckerton. He was surprising us with a trip to the Truck-erton Food Truck Festival.

The next day, Pop came early. He said he was meeting my grandmother at Wildflowers, Too that evening, so we could just run down for a few hours.

"Wait, I remember Wildflowers, Too," I said. "My mom took us there. It was in Yardville."

"Wasn't the owner a woman named Amanda?" asked T-Bone. "They had awesome food."

"They sure do," said Pop. "We're meeting a couple of friends there, so I'm under strict instructions not to eat too much and spoil my appetite."

"You're on your own," T-Bone laughed. "I'm going to eat so much, you'll have to roll me home. My mom gave me $100.00 to treat everyone."

"$100.00?" I asked. "That's a lot of money for four people eating healthy, isn't it?"

"She wasn't sure how many people were going," said T-Bone. "So she said to give you the rest for gas and any tolls."

With Pop driving, there were no tolls. He must have known every back road and byway in the state. We went around Joint Base McGuire-Dix-Lakehurst to Pemberton. A couple of turns later we were on Route 72 and then a right turn onto Route 539.

"Uh, did you forget something?" asked T-Bone.

"Don't think so," said Pop as he kept driving.

"You passed the Garden State Parkway entrance," he pointed out.

"Well Tommy, Tuckerton is straight ahead," Pop laughed. "We'll make a right on Route 9 and be at the Tuckerton Seaport in a few minutes."

"Oh, I guess that way works," T-Bone conceded. The traffic on Route 9 was very heavy, but for some reason, Pop didn't make that right turn he had mentioned. He continued on Route 539.

"Whatcha doin?" I asked. "Now, did you forget something?"

"No, no, I didn't forget anything," he said with a smile. "We have to make one stop first."

He drove until we reached Bass Avenue.

"Oh, I know where we're going," I proudly announced. "Isn't this the street where Captain Cliff and Patti live?"

"Patti does," he said, "Cliff passed a while ago."

"That's sad," said T-Bone. "I would have liked to have met him."

"He definitely would have gotten a kick out of you, Tommy," my grandfather said with a smile. "He had a funny way of tapping his forehead with the palm of his hand and saying 'Geez' when he heard weird or strange things."

"One afternoon with T-Bone and he would have had a concussion," said Wanda.
"Why are we stopping here?" I asked, as we pulled up the stone driveway.

"When I told your grandmother I was running down here with you kids, she asked me to stop by and check on her," he said. "She also wanted me to give her this candle she found at a yard sale."

I looked in the gift bag that rested on the console and saw a big, pink jar candle.

"Hey Pop, I think this candle was used," I warned him. "You might want to take it back before you give it to Patti as a gift."

"No, no," he laughed. "Your grandmother found that candle at a yard sale. The husband of the woman she bought it from was allergic to it."

"I don't get it," I said. "Why not get her a new one?"

"Look at the label," he said.

I pulled the candle out of the tissue paper and

looked at the label. It said *Roses of Cliffwalk*. I wondered if it had something to do with Captain Cliff. It turned out I was right. That was Patti's favorite fragrance and it was discontinued. My grandmother, a huge Yankee Candle fan, always asked about it, in case it returned. She kept an eye out for it at yard sales and garage sales and happened to get lucky.

We rang the doorbell and Patti appeared, holding her dog, Coral. My grandmother definitely knew what she was doing. As soon as Patti pulled out the candle, she started to cry. Pop gave her a hug, they told a few funny Cliff stories, and then we headed to the food trucks.

The festival was really exciting. There was music and every kind of food you could imagine. I was starting to wonder if T-Bone's mom actually sent enough money. I wanted to try everything. We wandered from truck to truck, buying a couple of things at each one and sharing. We decided to take bites of everything so we could sample as much as possible. It was fantastic and the atmosphere was really fun. It also didn't hurt that the sun was shining and there was a light breeze.

"What do you say, kids?" Pop asked as we got close to a cupcake truck. "We better go before my wife finds out I ate too much!"

"Good idea," said T-Bone, "but the rest of us aren't married, so I'll be right back."

T-Bone disappeared and then reappeared holding a cardboard box. It had five giant cupcakes.

"Why five?" I asked.

"Me, you, Wanda, and Pop," he said.

"That's only four people," I said, a little confused.

"Two are for your grandfather," he explained.

"Are you kidding?" I asked. "He'll get in trouble if he eats one cupcake. You heard what my grand-mother said."

"That's exactly why I got the fifth cupcake," T-Bone grinned. *That's the one he's gonna give to your grandmother!"*

Chapter Eleven

First World Problems

When our school found out *Austin the Unstoppable* was coming, everyone was excited. We went on their website to prepare and they had student guides, teacher guides, pre-show activities, post-show activities, and physical activities. Luckily, Ms. Swanson handled everything for the show and the teachers took over the fair. All of our ideas were ready to go.

After school that day, Wanda asked how jump rope lessons were going. I confessed that I hadn't even started and she reminded me the fair was fast approaching. As Co-Presidents, they had to be prepared to try everything. If T-Bone was as bad at jumping rope as he said, it could be a disaster.

And, because T-Bone was so in love with Wanda, lessons would have to wait until she left.

A few minutes after Wanda unpacked her tote bag, T-Bone came running in. As usual, he was smelling like his dad. The only difference was that he was wearing a velvet workout suit that looked like something an old man might wear. Making it even worse, he was wearing a thick sweat band around his head. He looked like a velvet nightmare from the 1980s.

"Whatcha wearing?" I asked.

"Well, I thought about it, and I need help jumping rope," he admitted. "Like a lot of help."

"Okay," said Wanda, trying to avoid embarrassing him. "I'll talk to you guys later."

"Where are you going?" he asked her.

"I thought you were gonna, um, *train*," she said.

"You can stay," he shrugged. "This job might be bigger than Nicky."

"Are you sure?" she asked.

"Might as well," he said. "Let's get started. Oh, wait, I almost forgot."

We weren't sure what he had forgotten, and waited patiently while he rummaged through a tote bag. I didn't notice the bag when he came in. I'm not sure how I missed it, though. It was pink with big, bright red lips. In neon letters, it read Hot Lips.

"Whatcha got there?" I asked, trying not to laugh.

"What? The bag?" he asked. "It's my mom's activity bag. She used to use it for her aerobics classes and for roller blading."

"When? In 1986?" I asked.

"Someone's a little jealous," he said as he strapped on a pink helmet, elbow pads and knee pads.

"Yeah, that's what it is," I replied, trying harder not to laugh. "It's a shame your mom wasn't a hockey goalie. They wear bigger pads."

"But do they wear these?" he asked as he pulled two lavender leg warmers over his calves.

"I sure hope not," I said, tears welling up in my eyes.

I glanced over at Wanda and noticed the same wide-eyed look of shock on her face. Positive that I couldn't hold in the laughter a second longer, I ran upstairs to get the jump rope. When I was safely in my room, I closed the door, put a towel over my face, and laughed. Once I composed myself, I grabbed the jump rope and calmly walked back down. But, one look at T-Bone's pink helmet, elbow pads, knee pads, lavender leg warmers, headband, and velvet outfit sent me running back upstairs. I felt bad leaving Wanda, but this was an *every man for himself* situation.

Eventually, we all went out to the back yard and I wondered how to start. I wasn't sure if he should try it first, or if I should teach him first. I asked him and he grabbed the jump rope.

With a death grip on the wooden handles, he took a deep breath and the rest was a blur. It was like his arms and legs were fighting one another. One moment he was counting to three and the next, he was a twisted jump rope mess, flat on the ground.

"T-Bone!" Wanda shrieked. "Are you okay?"

"I'm fine," he mumbled.

"What just happened?" I asked, trying to untangle him. It happened so fast that I would have needed slow motion to figure it out.

"I told you that I can't jump rope," he said.

"No one would imagine it'd be that bad," I said.

I honestly didn't know where to start. I decided we should start slow by holding the handles and swinging the rope over his head, without jumping. Somehow he even managed to turn that into a disaster. For an hour, we tried to help him and then we gave up. We were afraid he would break his neck if he tried anymore.

"Why don't we check the questionnaire results?" I suggested, trying to provide a diversion.

Just as we were about to go inside, Maggie came out, saw the jump rope, grabbed it, and started jumping, and jumping fast. Not only did she jump fast, she sang a song about being *down in a valley where the green grass grows*. T-Bone stopped and studied her movements. When she put the rope down, he grabbed it and started singing the song. Unfortunately, the song wasn't the answer.

Looking over the answers, it was clear why we

have an obesity problem: too much confusion, too many choices, and too little time.

"You know," said Wanda, "the Austin show will probably clear up a lot of the confusion. Between the show, and the activities they offer, many of the things kids don't understand should make sense.

"True," I said.

Later that day, we headed over to George's house. After we moved some boxes for him and straightened up his garage, we told him about all of our plans. He was really impressed.

"You know what these problems are?" he asked.

"Big and complicated?" I suggested.

"First world problems," he replied. "We're a nation with so much and we can't seem to handle it. There are many places that have catastrophic shortages of clean water and food. We have so much and so much of our time, energy, and money is dedicated to dealing with the problem of having too much."

"But there are so many hungry people right here in our country," I said.

"That's the other tragedy," he nodded. "You can live in one of the wealthiest countries in the world and many people, even kids, still go to bed hungry at night."

"What's the answer?" asked T-Bone.

"Well, like most problems, it's complicated," he began. "So much needs attention, but I think what we need most is an understanding of what poverty really is. You can't solve a problem if you don't understand it. Many Americans live very close to the poverty line and don't know it. Then, you have to make people see that dealing with poverty is in everyone's best interest and best for our country."

"I'm a kid and I even know that," said T-Bone. "Poverty costs everyone money. If we invested in really fixing it, then more people would be contributing and it would cost everyone less."

"Very insightful," said George.

"Wanda told us this when she made poverty her cause," T-Bone admitted. "First, we learned how poverty affected education and literacy. Now, we're learning that poverty affects health, too."

"Exactly," said George. "Limited income means

limited transportation and limited chances to select fresh and healthy foods at grocery stores."

"Yeah, it's not cheap to eat healthy," I agreed.

Before we left, we re-invited him to the Fitness Fun Fair and he said he'd bring a surprise.

Before we knew it, the big day had arrived. The Austin cast and crew were all set up and ready to enlighten our school. The show was great and many kids could relate to Austin, a junk food junkie who was addicted to video games. When they showed the 19-teaspoons of sugar in soda, the whole audience gasped. But the best part of the show was the humor and the music. The writers were clever and creative. If they had just stood there and told us this was bad and that was bad, we wouldn't have been inspired. In fact, most kids wouldn't have even paid attention. The way they delivered the message was definitely memorable.

The students and teachers all clapped wildly when it was over. Because we told Ms. Swanson about the show, she invited us backstage to meet the cast. They were as great backstage as they were on-stage. We told them about the questionnaire and how they cleared up much of the confusion.

We also told them about my dad and how we all came together, like Austin did, for his mom. They seemed really touched, especially Barry Wyner and Daniel Israel, the writers. I wanted to tell them how clever, creative, and brilliant the show was. I wanted to tell them how impressive it was. What I actually did was nod and smile.

"What would you like the impact of the show to be?" asked Wanda. I wondered why I couldn't think of such good questions under pressure.

"Well," said Barry, "I strongly hope that this musical inspires young people to form healthy habits. Kids are dreamers, and they each have such potential. But, they must be healthy enough to make those dreams come true. You can't neglect your health and expect anything good to happen. Lifestyle habits and eating habits directly affect the course of a person's life, for better or worse, so I hope this musical helps kids make good choices."

"I like that you make learning fun," I finally said.

"So do we," Daniel nodded. "No one ever said that learning has to be boring!"

"Exactly," said T-Bone. "How many kids do you think you've reached?"

"Well," said Barry, "we keep growing each year and we've toured hundreds of schools and reached tens of thousands of students."

"That's incredible," I nodded.

"Look who's talking," said a man as he entered the room. "Hi, I'm Jim Jack and I'm the Education and Outreach Director at the George Street Playhouse. I have to say, you kids are doing amazing work."

Apparently, Mrs. Leary and Ms. Swanson told them about our work. He said we were very similar because we're sharing important information. I couldn't believe he knew about us. When we told him about how we were trying to provide kids with facts so they could make their own decisions, they all high-fived us. They even noticed the signs and charts around the building reminding everyone to be healthy and track their activities, sleep, and steps. We told them that since we started tracking our steps, we kept increasing them each day.

"That's the idea," Jim said with a smile.

When they left the building, we felt like we had done a really good thing. Now, that we had kicked off our big be healthy initiative, we had one more big activity – *the fair.*

We met with Mr. B. and Mr. J. to plan the physical activities. We planned an obstacle course, a jump rope section, a run the bases area, a dance area, and plenty of room for a game that I invented called *Healthy Says*. It was really just Simon Says, but instead of saying Simon Says, the leader said Healthy Says. And instead of touching your head, you would jog in place or do jumping jacks and other physical activities. Because our list of activities had grown so large, we decided to move the foods to the cafeteria. It would leave more room in the gym and allow people to sit at tables and eat.

Mrs. Leary had a last minute suggestion to setup tables in the hallways to highlight good choices. I wasn't sure what she meant at first, but she wanted to put up fact tables. Each table would have facts about choices some people make. Some of the topics she suggested were smoking, alcohol, drugs, medicine, sleep, and stress. I thought it was a great idea since middle school is where some kids start making bad choices. Presenting them with facts might give them something to think about.

As the fair crept closer, our school was buzzing with excitement. *Austin* was definitely a great kickoff event. Each day leading up to the fair, the morning announcements included a healthy tip. Wanda was busy working on the food demonstrations and my mom offered to help her prepare them and come up with fun ideas. That night, Wanda and T-Bone came by and we all sat in the kitchen planning visual presentations.

"Wanda, I have a great idea," my mom began, "let's get several beverages and stack the sugar cubes in front of each one. But, also give them alternatives."

"That's a great idea," said Wanda. "We can use the Fooducate app to find better alternatives."

"Exactly," she nodded. "Then I thought we could take foods that have confusing serving sizes and line them up. Kids would have to guess how many servings are in each sample."

"Brilliant," Wanda agreed. "Maybe we should take common foods we eat at home with three different sizes to see if they know the actual portion size."

"Yes," my mom smiled and high-fived her. "That's perfect. So we covered sugar, serving sizes, and portions; what else should we do?"

"How about ingredients?" I suggested.

"Ooh, that gives me an idea," said my mom. "Let's take cookies, muffins, macaroni and cheese, and soups and list the ingredients for both homemade and store-bought to show the difference."

"I love it," said Wanda. "We can print them and put them on poster board with pictures of the foods."

"And don't forget that demonstration you did in my kitchen, moving the foods into healthy rows."

"Good one," said Wanda.

Then suddenly, we heard a noise from the back yard. It was faint at first; then there was a banging and clanging. Then the faint noise, again. We all stopped talking and moved toward the window.

"Is that what I think it is?" I asked Wanda.

"I think so," she whispered.

My mom quietly slid the window open so we could hear. And there it was, T-Bone singing *Down in the Valley* while trying to jump rope. My mom and Wanda covered their mouths at the same time and looked at one another. A moment later, he crashed into the garbage cans, again.

"Oh, Nicky," my mom gasped, "go help him."

"Mom, about that," I laughed. "I think he's beyond help."

"Nicky, why is he practicing?" she asked. "He's not planning on jumping rope at the fair, is he?"

"He probably is," I said. "But I don't know how to help. He's a mess as soon as he touches the rope."

"There must be something we can do," she said as he crashed into Maggie and Emma's toys. "Can we at least call him in to help?"

"You can try," said Wanda.

My mom opened the back door and looked for him. For a moment she didn't see him and she didn't hear him. Then she saw a figure emerge from the bushes.

"Tommy, can you give us a hand with the food demonstrations?" she said.

"Sure, Mrs. A.," he replied.

"You know, kids, I was thinking," said my mom, "maybe you should all split the duties at the fair. Like, Wanda you stay with the demonstrations and fact tables, Nicky you stay with the activities, and Tommy, maybe you should man the foods."

I was sure my mom was too obvious and that T-Bone would know she was trying to steer him away from the jump ropes.

"Good idea," he said. "But maybe we should switch stations."

"No, no," my mom shook her head. "It's better to be the expert at one than to know a little about all."

"That's a good idea," he said, "but if we do that, we won't all see everything."

There was no way around it. T-Bone would somehow end up in the gym and he would somehow end up with a jump rope in his hand. And then he would somehow humiliate himself. My mom was torn between hurting his feelings and letting him embarrass himself. She decided to do what she did when we were little kids. She told a similar story.

"You know, Tommy, I'm so glad you're focused on wellness," she began. "It's so important. I know when I was a kid, I wanted to ice skate so badly. My mom kept taking me, but instead of getting better, each time, I got worse. It was the craziest thing. I just could not get better. Isn't that weird?"

"Not really," he said. "You gave up too quick."

"Maybe," she said, trying to get him to quit, "or maybe there are just some people who will never, as hard as they try, learn certain activities."

"I don't agree," he said. "I think you should never give up. You just quit too soon."

My mom looked at me and Wanda and shrugged.

"T-Bone, you can't jump rope," said Wanda.

"What?" he asked.

"You cannot jump rope, not now, not ever," she repeated. "It's just not going to happen."

"What do you mean?" he asked, as if he had no idea what she was talking about. "I'm getting closer."

"The only thing you're getting closer to is a trip to the Emergency Room and a full body cast," she said. "Seriously, you are not making this easy."

"Are you implying that I can't jump rope?" he asked.

"No, I'm not implying it," she said. "I'm coming

right out and saying it. Listen, I'm your friend and I don't want to see you make a giant fool out of yourself or end up in the Emergency Room."

Before he could answer, she was in the pantry with my mom. T-Bone suddenly had the biggest smile on his face.

"What are you smiling about?" I asked, wondering why he wasn't upset by Wanda's comments.

"Are you kidding?" he asked.

"No, seriously," I insisted, "why are you smiling?"

"Did you hear what she said?" he asked. "Did you hear it?"

"Yes, I did," I nodded. "Did you?"

"I sure did," he said. "And do you know what that means? *She really cares about me.*"

Chapter Twelve

Down in the Valley

The day before the fair was just as hectic as the day before CODE READ, when we donated and delivered thousands of books to the kids in the Trenton Public Schools. There was so much to do and so many people hard at work. The art teacher decorated the cafeteria with flags from around the world, the gym looked fun and exciting and the fact tables looked like a professional had set them up. Well, it basically was professionals...it was Wanda and the teachers.

We all met in the cafeteria and discussed the schedule and how the day would unfold. Rosa, Matthew, Marlon and Sahara had volunteered to help and were in the gym blowing up balloons.

When they came in, I handed them copies of the schedule. They'd be working the cafeteria with their parents and talking about their heritage.

By the time we got home, I was exhausted, but I couldn't sleep. I was way too excited. I kept going over all of the things we needed to do and hoped I didn't forget anything. When the alarm went off, I felt like I had just closed my eyes.

The only good thing about being so busy is that I didn't have time to worry about my dad. Even though I knew he'd be okay, I was still worried. I didn't know how having Type 2 diabetes would affect him. I wondered if he'd be as active, more tired, or eventually need needles. This project, that T-Bone called *The Road to Wellness,* was the best thing we could have done.

I grabbed some fruit and yogurt, my mom's new weekday breakfast plan, and waited by the front door. Luckily, my mom offered to drive us to school early so we could make sure everything was ready. When we walked outside, Wanda and T-Bone were standing on our porch and Wanda was carrying two shopping bags filled with vegetable trays.

"Good morning," said my mom. "I thought we were picking you up."

"We thought we'd save you time," said T-Bone.

"Oh, okay," she said. "So is everyone excited?"

We all said yes, even though it was through yawns. I knew once we got there, we would all perk up. I was definitely relieved that T-Bone wasn't wearing one of his usual goofy outfits. Whenever we had something important to do, he arrived in a silly outfit. Today he just looked like himself.

Even though we arrived super early, the building was still busy. The custodians and several teachers were doing some last minute touch-ups. I had to admit it, the school looked better than I imagined. The cafeteria looked like Epcot! Rosa and Matthew stood with their parents as the cafeteria staff placed their trays in the ovens to keep them warm. We were excited to meet and thank their parents.

T-Bone went right over to them and introduced us. Mr. and Mrs. Kim were very friendly and took the time to explain everything they made and all of the ingredients. They also thanked us for teaching kids to be healthy.

Next, we met Mrs. Diaz, Rosa's mom. She smiled as much as Rosa and kept thanking us for inviting her. We told her we were just as excited to share healthy dishes from around the world as she was to make them. By the time we were done speaking, she had invited T-Bone over for dinner.

While we waited for Marlon and his dad, Sahara and her mom walked in. We could smell the chicken immediately and it smelled awesome. Mrs. Patel said she hoped she had made enough and when we saw her six large trays come in, we told her she had made plenty.

I decided to grab my cereal buffet and set up the bowls to demonstrate serving sizes and Wanda started setting up her veggie and dip trays.

"Nicky," she said, "I don't think we'll have enough veggies and dip."

"What?" I asked. "You brought tons. We're fine."

"I don't know," she shook her head.

I had never seen Wanda panic. This was a first.

As set-up continued, we met Marlon's dad, Mr. Harris. I could smell the pineapple and knew Ms. Swanson's International Flair at the Fair idea was a winner. We were offering kids healthy choices and a glimpse into some healthy dishes from around the world. Even better, they had a chance to speak to people from other cultures.

There was a buzz in the room, and it quickly turned into a conga line. Marlon's dad turned on some Jamaican music and everyone was dancing around, even the parents. Mr. and Mrs. Kim grabbed a broom to start a limbo and Sahara's mom was first in line. She was able to go lower than anyone, except Rosa and her mom. They were unbelievable. Everyone was clapping and the mood was electric. What a great way to start, I thought.

A moment later, a familiar face walked in. It was Mrs. Rizzo, T-Bone's mom, followed by his three older brothers, each carrying a giant crockpot full of Garden Minestrone soup. I had never seen all of T-Bone's brothers at the same time before. It was crazy how much they all looked alike. I laughed when I wondered what my dad would do if he saw four T-Bone's walk into a room, especially if that room was our kitchen. Once they set up the crock pots, they joined the limbo line. Who knew the Rizzo's weren't so flexible. One by one, each brother landed flat on his back. T-Bone's mom stood there shaking her head. T-Bone's un-coordination was now easier to understand; much, much easier.

About 30 minutes before we were scheduled to

begin, another familiar face walked in. It was George and he was carrying three long silver pans.

"Hey, George," I said. "Thanks for coming."

"My pleasure, kiddo," he said with a wink. "The place looks great."

"Hey George," said T-Bone. "Let me take those trays from you."

"There's more in the car," he said.

"More?" I asked. "You didn't have to do all of that."

"Well, I made about 200 mini fruit kabobs with super fruits," he proudly explained.

"Wow, thanks," I said. "Do you have time to stay?"

"Wouldn't miss it," he nodded. "Put me to work."

"You may regret that," I laughed.

"It's good to feel needed," he said with a wink.

Wanda, T-Bone, and I grabbed her clipboard and did a final walk through. Hot foods? Check. Plates, bowls, forks, spoons, napkins, waters? Check.

Fruit kabobs and veggie trays? Check. Fact tables? Check. Activity stations? Check. Tracking sheets? Check.

I found Mrs. Swanson standing near the main office and gave her a thumbs up. The office figured out a way to send large groups throughout the day. Luckily, it was only a half day.

When the first groups came down they started sampling foods and filling out comment cards. The cafeteria really did look like Epcot. Students were having long conversations with the parents who prepared the international meals and I saw George talking to students and staff. I grabbed a plate and tried a piece of everything. I had never really tried foods from other cultures before and I surprised myself. Everything they prepared was amazing. It's no wonder everyone was raving about the food.

Down the hall, every Fact Table was crowded with kids. The teachers, volunteers, and students working each table didn't preach or lecture, they just provided facts. I really believed that if most kids had the facts, they would make the good choices.

The smoking table showed the impact of smoking on your body, from your lungs and heart, to the risks for most cancers, to wrinkles and loss of teeth.

The alcohol table showed how long it takes an adult to process a drink and the many impacts of drinking, including the number of people who died each year in drunk driving crashes.

There was a sunscreen table that provided pictures and statistics about sun exposure. Wanda even included information about tanning beds. She also included how often sunscreen needs to be applied. Spoiler alert: way more than anyone thought.

The Oral Health table gave lots of great tips for dental health. I never understood the importance of gum health until now. A bunch of teachers chipped in and bought mini-flossers for kids to try out. Since so many people avoided flossing, these little flossers made it easy. There were pictures of cavities and healthy gums and videos showing how to brush the right way. It turned out most people missed a bunch of teeth and didn't brush as long as they should have. I was probably guilty of that when I was in a hurry. I was sure that I'd never do that again. I wanted my teeth to last my whole life.

As I made my way through the hallway, I noticed a table for BEAM. I went up and introduced myself to a woman at the table. She told me her name was Susan Haspel and she was the State Director of the Boys and Girls Clubs in New Jersey. Her fact table was very impressive and kids seemed anxious to stop by. Even if they didn't have asthma, they knew someone who did. I wondered how Susan even knew about our fair and she said that Mr. B. invited her.

The next table had a large banner for Healthy U. I introduced myself to the woman behind the table and, surprisingly, her name was Susan, also. Her name was Sue Cornell and she was the State Director for the New Jersey YMCA State Alliance. A moment later, a gentleman appeared. His name was Bill Lovett and he was the Executive Director of the New Jersey YMCA State Alliance. They were very friendly and really happy to answer questions and even shared some great tips and ideas. When a student asked what advice she would give kids, she told them to never be afraid to try something new, whether it was a new sport, a new game, or even a new food.

"I should take your advice," I admitted. "I'm never quick to try new foods."

"Well, think of it this way," she said. "You should eat to nourish your body and to give you energy, especially your brain. Trying new foods gives you more potential ways to do that."

"Good point," I said. "My friends and I decided to try to be more active. Except our one friend is, let's just say, coordination challenged."

"You know, that's the great thing about physical activity," she began, "it's not about being good at a sport, it's about finding joy in playing and being active – things like sports, dancing, biking, hiking, exploring, and even jumping rope."

"That's funny," I laughed, "the friend I was talking about cannot jump rope to save his life."

"It can't be that bad," said Bill, somewhat shocked. "As bad as you can imagine it, multiplied by 10!" I explained.

When I thanked them, they said they were happy to be there. I told them the feeling was mutual. Every table had a wellness-themed topic. One of the most popular tables was actually the social media table. Our tech teachers had put together a great display that explained just how permanent the internet was. She told us that even tiny things posted on the internet live there forever, even pictures and comments. With screen shots, nothing could ever be permanently deleted. She also told us that colleges and employers check people out online. Many people have not been accepted to their dream school or hired for their dream job because of pictures or comments they posted years earlier. I didn't have time for social media, but if I ever did, I would use my mother's rule: never do or say anything I couldn't do or say in front of my grandparents.

My next stop was the demonstration tables. I watched everyone try to figure out serving sizes and portion sizes. They were shocked every time they were wrong, which seemed like almost every time. The Ingredients Fact Table was actually funny. Listening to everyone try to pronounce the ingredients was hysterical.

A moment later, I heard my name on the loud speaker. I headed toward the office, wondering what had gone wrong. Hopefully, T-Bone hadn't tried to jump rope. When I walked in, Mrs. Leary was standing with four people I didn't recognize.

"Oh, there you are," Mrs. Leary said with a big smile. "I'd like to introduce you to some guests that I invited."

"Hi," I said, not sure what to do next.

"So, everyone, this is Nicky," she said. "Nicky, this is Don and Jean from the Horizon Foundation, Mr.

Steve Kalafer from the Somerset Patriots, and over here, we have Morgan Hoffman."

"Holy cow!" I shrieked. "I mean, um, holy, um…"

"It's okay," said Mrs. Leary. "And don't worry, Nicky. T-Bone and Wanda are coming."

"Did I hear my name?" asked T-Bone, walking in and followed by Wanda.

I don't know why she didn't call them first, I thought. My first words were a mumble jumble of nonsense, while they were completely smooth. Don and Jean thanked us for promoting wellness, an issue near and dear to their hearts. They introduced us to Mr. Kalafer and T-Bone called him Mr. *Healthy Plate*. Thankfully, T-Bone didn't insult him. Then we met Morgan Hoffman. I couldn't believe a real PGA golfer was at our school and, more importantly, at our fair. The first thing we did was thank Morgan for responding to our letter.

T-Bone, of course, had questions for Steve Kalafer and waited about six seconds before he began.

"Do you really own a baseball team?" he asked. "Do you like baseball? Do you ever go to the games? Is *baseball owner* your real job?"

"I do own the team," he began, "but I'm also the Founding Chairman and owner of Flemington Car & Truck Country. Oh, and yes, I love baseball. My family and I attend about 50 games each year."

"Wow," T-Bone replied. "Is it fun to own a team?"

"Tremendous fun," he winked.

"I have a question," said Wanda. "How do you feel about the *Healthy Plate* initiative?"

"Actually," he said, very seriously, "it's the single most important statement at TD Bank Ballpark. I'm very proud to be a part of it."

"You're very successful," noticed T-Bone. "Are you a pharmacist? I want to be one when I grow up."

"He means *philanthropist*," Wanda corrected.

"Oh," Steve laughed. "Well, yes, I've been very blessed and I support many causes, but I usually don't talk about it."

"Classy," said T-Bone. "Very classy."

"Do you have advice for kids?" asked Wanda, remembering the great advice Morgan gave us.

"Well, I'd say to be kind, work hard, make money, be fair, do good, and *exercise*," he smiled.

"Words to live by," Wanda nodded. "Thank you."

We gave them the royal tour of the fair and they were really impressed. The putting station was set up in the hallway so we could control the crowd. It turned out to be a great idea as the line wrapped all the way down the hall. Morgan seemed really happy to see so many kids in line to golf and even happier when Mrs. Leary brought him to the front of the line. He was so good, he practically put on a seminar. When he passed the club to Steve and Don, they easily sunk the ball. When it was Jean's turn, T-Bone offered to show her how to do it. He took the putter and hit the ball, and hit the ball, and hit the ball. After five consecutive misses, Jean asked if she might have a try. As if Karma had been watching from the sidelines, Jean's putt went up the hill, around the edge of the cup, and then, plunk, right inside. Being a good sport, T-Bone high-fived her.

At the end of the tour, our guests decided to visit our international cafe. We thanked them for coming and for all of their work to improve wellness and returned to our stations.

About an hour later, I maneuvered through the crowds and finally made it to the gym. The room felt electric. Kids were playing games and dancing. It was amazing. I walked over to the run-the-bases game and they were having more fun than if they were playing video games. I even heard one kid ask who had invented the game. Toward the back of the gym, I heard Mr. B. leading a game of Healthy Says. I saw everyone marching in place until he yelled, "Healthy says hop." Suddenly the entire group was hopping. I did a double take when I saw the head custodian and my bus driver hopping, too. The excitement was contagious.

The biggest shock of all, was when I looked at the obstacle course, and there, racing on two scooters and laughing uncontrollably, were my parents. I didn't even know they were coming. And cheering on the sideline was Timmy, Maggie, and Emma.

Most kids would see their parents playing and think it was funny. I looked at my parents and all I felt was relief. Seeing my dad having so much fun and joining in, I realized that diabetes or no diabetes, he was the same old dad. *But if I were diabetes, I would be scared because diabetes' days were definitely numbered.*

A moment later, I saw Timmy, Maggie, and Emma

over at the dance section. They were having so much fun that they didn't even realize they were exercising. Suddenly, I had a scary thought and looked to see where T-Bone was. I hoped he wasn't near the jump rope section. I scanned the gym and spotted him. He was heading directly toward the jump ropes. I tried to beat him, but the crowd was too thick. This was such a good day, the last thing we needed was T-Bone flailing around with a jump rope. By the time I got there, he had the jump rope in his hand and was heading toward Wanda. I saw him whisper in her ear and then, she actually smiled.

No, no, I thought. What's she doing? Why isn't she stopping him? I couldn't believe she'd let him make a fool out of himself in front of everyone.

But then, the strangest thing happened. He held onto one end of the rope and tossed the other end to Wanda. A moment later, I saw Maggie and Emma holding hands and jumping while Wanda and T-Bone twirled the rope. While they all sang *Down in the Valley*, T-Bone sang the loudest.

Phew, I thought. That was a close one.

When the first bell rang, everyone went back to their classes to get ready for dismissal and we started cleaning up. Mr. B., Mr. J., Mrs. Leary, and Ms. Swanson came over to where T-Bone and I were standing. They all seemed very happy.

"Boys, congratulations," said Ms. Swanson.

"Really," said Mr. B., "great job. Fantastic event."

"You done good," said Mr. J. as he patted my head. "You've really made a big impact."

Mrs. Leary just smiled and nodded in agreement.

"Boys, there's someone who wants to meet you," said Ms. Swanson.

"Oh, we already met them," said T-Bone.

"Them?" asked Ms. Swanson.

"Yup," said T-Bone. "Don, Jean, Steve, and Morgan."

"Actually, it's someone else," she said with a smile.

"Oh, no," T-Bone said as he turned to me and Wanda. "Do you think it's Billy or the Governor, here to elevate us to Official Junior Ambassadors? How could they surprise us? I don't have my suit!"

"T-Bone, we're not being elevated," said Wanda.

"Seriously?" he whispered. "What do we have to do to become official? We promote NJ, we discuss poverty, environment, and government, we started CODE READ to donate thousands of books. Now, we're trying to save lives. Why don't they notice?"

"I noticed all of your hard work," said a woman with a big smile. "I actually know all about you."

"Boys, this is Heather Tedesco, from Celebrate New Jersey. Heather this is Nicky, Tommy, and Wanda," said Ms. Swanson. "These are the kids I told you about."

"It's nice to meet you," she said, as she shook our hands. "You really did an amazing job today!"

"Thanks," we all said. "It's nice to meet you, too."

"So, Ms. Swanson filled me in on what you're doing," she began. "I'm blown away. Your devotion to New Jersey and good causes is outstanding."

"Thanks," I said. "But you have an outstanding program, too. Ms. Swanson told us all about it."

"I appreciate that," she smiled. "Since our work is

so similar, we should work together on a project. I was thinking of CRUNCH BUNCH."

"We'd love to," said Wanda.

"I want you to check something else out," she said. "When you get home, look up the New Jersey State Governor's Jefferson Awards for Public Service."

"What's that?" asked T-Bone.

"I think the name is pretty self-explanatory," Wanda said as she nudged him.

"Well, I'm the Regional Director for Students in Action," she explained. "We recognize outstanding public service, including acts conducted by youth."

"Like a Hall of Fame?" asked T-Bone, perking up.

"Well," she said, "in a way, yes. Except we don't recognize people for being famous, we honor people who perform selfless acts of service."

"That's us," said T-Bone. "And we're still unofficial."

"Well, I suspect you don't do all of the good things you do for the glory," she said.

"Of course, not," Wanda and I said together.

"I also suspect that you continue to get involved because you see how much people appreciate your work," she continued. "Am I right?"

"Yeah," T-Bone nodded. "I know I shouldn't be so worried about becoming official."

"Well, I wouldn't feel too bad about it," she said. "It would be an exciting and unique recognition, but the work you're doing is even bigger than a title."

"I'd like to hear more about the awards," Wanda said.

"Well, people are nominated for exemplifying volunteerism and service," she began. "Sometimes it's individuals and sometimes it's groups."

"It sounds like a great program," said Wanda.

"Oh, it is," she continued. "In fact, one award in particular might interest you. A 14-year-old young man named Lawrence Raia realized kids didn't enjoy pleasure reading. At 15-years-old, he decided to encourage 7th and 8th graders to read so he approached two schools, one in East Harlem and one in Newark, to start an afterschool book club."

"Sounds like a kid with great ideas," I said.

"It gets better," she went on, "he started Raia Reads, partnering with K-8 schools, donating over 500 copies. He even gets local authors involved!"

"Awesome," said Wanda. "We took stands for issues like poverty, education and reading. We know how hard it is to create a valuable program." "Absolutely," said Heather. "That's why we think it's important to recognize people for their efforts, and also to provide examples to inspire others. If you'd like to come to the awards ceremony and be really inspired, I'd love to have you as my guests."

"That would be awesome," said T-Bone, totally forgetting about his recent disappointment.

"Definitely," Wanda and I said together.

"Great, here's my card," she said. "Once you recover from this event, email me and we can see about combining our resources."

"Okay, thanks," said T-Bone.

As the gym emptied out, we went to the cafeteria to help the parent volunteers clean up.

"Rosa, Matthew, Sahara, and Marlon," said Wanda, "thanks for everything you did today."

"No problem," said Marlon. "My dad had a good time. He was singing and dancing all morning."

"My parents did, too," said Matthew. "If you need help with any other projects, let me know."

"Thanks," said T-Bone. "We can always use help."

"Then count me in, too," said Rosa. "This was fun. My mom said she'll help, also."

"Wow," said Wanda, "that's fantastic."

"My mom and I both had a really good time," said Sahara. "She loves to share her Indian cooking."

"You guys are great," I said. "You and your parents made this event so much better than it would have been. We'd love to have you help us again."

When everything was cleaned up, we went to say goodbye to George. We looked all over and finally, there he was, shooting baskets with Mr. B.

"This guy is great," said Mr. B. as he passed George the ball. "But, I think he's a ringer."

At first I thought they were just taking some shots, but then I realized they were playing HORSE. While no one was paying attention, we heard singing and then a big thud. We turned around, and once again, saw T-Bone tangled up in the rope.

"Great job," said Mr. B. "Excellent tutoring."

"It's not my fault," I laughed. "He's hopeless."

"Nicky, take over," said George. "I left off on R."

A moment later, T-Bone and George walked into the hallway. Just as I got crushed finishing George's game of HORSE, I heard a loud scream. Mr. B. and I looked at each other and thought something must have happened to George.

We ran out of the gym and down the hallway to see the most shocking sight I had ever seen. With a handkerchief wrapped around his eyes and singing *Down in the Valley*, T-Bone was jumping rope.

"No way!" I exclaimed. "How'd you teach him?"

"Easy," he laughed as T-Bone faded from sight.

"No, seriously," I said. "How'd you do that?"

"That kid thinks about things too much," George explained. "He needed a few less distractions, so I blindfolded him."

"Well, it's working perfectly," I laughed.

Then, suddenly, we heard a crash and a splash at the same time. T-Bone crashed into the custodian's bucket and dumped the water all over the floor. With the floor covered in water, T-Bone slid down the hallway, finally crashing into a locker.

"I'm okay. I'm okay," he yelled. "And, don't worry, this time it wasn't the jump rope. *This time it was the bucket.*"

Nicky Fifth's New Jersey Contest

Are You A New Jersey Character?

Submit your favorite New Jersey destination to Nicky Fifth, T-Bone, and Wanda you could become a character in an upcoming Nicky Fifth book. Write a 3-4 paragraph persuasive essay, selling your idea to Nicky, T-Bone, and Wanda. Make sure your idea is located in New Jersey and hasn't been included in a previous book in the series. Check the website for a list of places already included.

Entries are judged on creativity, writing style, history, and level of persuasion. Do not list numerous locations; focus on one and make sure it is located in New Jersey. To enter, visit www.nickyfifth.com and be sure you have your parents' permission.

Prizes:

1st Prize - $200.00 Barnes & Noble Gift Card
YOUR idea is used in an upcoming book
YOU become a character in the book

2nd Prize - $100.00 Barnes & Noble Gift Card
YOUR idea is used in an upcoming book

3rd Prize - $75.00 Barnes & Noble Gift Card
YOUR idea is used in an upcoming book

Nicky Fifth's New Jersey
Contest Winners

1st Place - Eden Collins
Normandy Park School, Morristown, NJ
Fosterfields Farms

2nd Place - Tie- Fiona Fan
Stony Brook School, Hopewell, NJ
Duke Farms

2nd Place - Tie- Alex Boccumini
Stony Brook School, Hopewell, NJ
Duke Farms

2nd Place - Tie- Briana Mahilo
Stony Brook School, Hopewell, NJ
Duke Farms

3rd Place - Tie - Sarah Miller Piotrowski
Stony Brook School, Hopewell, NJ
Brothers Moon Restaurant

3rd Place - Tie - Matthew Desiderio
McKinley Avenue Elementary School, Manahawkin, NJ
Tuckerton

3rd Place - Tie - Nolan Friend
McKinley Avenue Elementary School, Manahawkin, NJ
Tuckerton

Nicky Fifth Curriculum

The Nicky Fifth Curriculum brings New Jersey and vital topics currently omitted from test-based curriculums to life. Through humorous, realistic fiction, the Nicky Fifth series allows teachers to present numerous topics to students within the context of literature, eliminating the need for additional instruction time. As opposed to current trends, the Nicky Fifth curriculum encourages teachers to embrace their creativity and adapt lessons to address the needs of their students.

Teachers can seamlessly combine literature with topics such as New Jersey history, geography, civics, government, the environment, the art of debate, education, poverty, and wellness in an age-appropriate manner. Using the familiar Nicky Fifth characters, this unique Jersey-centric curriculum spans grades 2-6, is easy to implement, is inexpensive, and easily lends itself to extension activities. Schools purchase the chapter books and Nicky Fifth provides amazing multi-discipline materials for all learners, at no cost.

Visit **nickyfifth.com** to easily access over 400 printable worksheets, dozens of slide shows, and exciting videos...*all at no cost!* Enjoy!

About the Nicky Fifth Foundation

In May 2015, after years of providing tens of thousands of free books to schools and children in need, Lisa Funari-Willever created the Nicky Fifth Foundation to promote literature, education, and awareness for New Jersey children.

With the help of her husband, Todd Willever, and good friend, Iris Hutchinson, the Nicky Fifth Foundation was born. The first step was establishing a dynamic Board of Directors to guide the foundation. Luckily, Lisa knew many dynamic people.

One by one, all of the board seats were enthusiastically occupied by individuals who really care about New Jersey kids. Along with Lisa, Todd, and Iris, the Board of Directors consists of Paula Agabiti, Karen Funari, Dawn Hiltner, Don Jay Smith, Walker Worthy, Brenda Zanoni, and Nancy Byrne.

Once the board was established, the first program, Nicky Fifth's CODE READ, began.

www.nickyfifth.org

About the Author,
Lisa Funari Willever

Lisa Funari Willever wanted to be an author since she was in the third grade and often says if there was a Guest Young Author contest when she was a child, she would have submitted a story a day. *Maybe two a day on weekends!*

She has been a wedding-dress-seller, a file clerk, a sock counter *(really)*, a hostess, waitress, teacher, and author. While she loved teaching in Trenton, New Jersey, becoming an author has been one of the most exciting adventures of her life. She is a full-time mom and a *night-time author* who travels all over the world visiting schools. She has been to hundreds of schools in dozens of states, including California, South Dakota, Iowa, South Carolina, North Carolina, Florida, Delaware, Connecticut, New York, Pennsylvania, West Virginia, Ohio, Nevada, Idaho, Utah, Alabama, Louisiana, and even the US Navy base in Sasebo, Japan.

Lisa has written over two dozen books for children and even a book for new teachers. Her critically acclaimed *Chumpkin* was selected as a favorite by First Lady Laura Bush and displayed at the White House, *Everybody Moos At Cows* was featured on the Rosie O'Donnell Show, and *Garden State Adventure* and *32 Dandelion Court* have been on the prestigious New Jersey Battle of the Books List. Some of her titles include *You Can't Walk A Fish, The Easter Chicken, Maximilian The Great, Where Do Snowmen Go?, The Culprit Was A Fly, Miracle on Theodore's Street, A Glove of Their Own, There's A Kid Under My Bed,* and *On Your Mark, Get Set, Teach.* Her Nicky Fifth series has been embraced by New Jersey schools and a unique and innovative Nicky Fifth curriculum has been developed.

Lisa is married to Todd Willever, a Captain in the Trenton Fire Department, and they have three children, Jessica, Patrick, and Timmy.

Lisa was a lifelong resident of Trenton and while she is proud to now reside in beautiful Mansfield Township, she treasures her 34 years in the city. She is a graduate of Trenton State College and loves nothing more than traveling with her family, reading, writing, and finding creative ways to avoid cooking!